THE ROBOT REVOLUTION

Carl Perrin

Carl Perrin (signature)

Sea Change Publications

Carl Perrin

This book is dedicated to Janet
Who has made all the difference

THE ROBOT REVOLUTION

Copyright © by Carl Perrin 2019

Carl Perrin

Table of Contents

Introduction

A Real Girl

A Custom-Made Android

If It Ain't One Thing

Microchips

Rip Van Winkle

Burying Ambrose

A Robot's Ransom

The Internet of Things

Harold's Robot Companion

Vote for Zandu

A Voice from Beyond

Baxter

Customer Service

The Office of Vital Statistics

Marrying Zelda

Chatbots

Too Sexy

How Like a God

Proposition 29

THE ROBOT REVOLUTION

Reconstituted Man
Double Trouble
Thelma and Louise
The History of Robots
Acknowledgements

Carl Perrin

Introduction

Robots! Chatbots! Artificial Intelligence! Machine Learning! New Technology! What is the world coming to?

It's coming to the Robot Revolution. That's what it's coming to. And how will we react when we see more and more robots in our daily life? Will we love them and want to marry them as Scott does in "Marrying Zelda"? Or want to hold a funeral for them when they break down and die as Frederick does in "Burying Ambrose"? Maybe some people will want to kidnap them as Francis and his sidekick do in "A Robot's Ransom." Others, no doubt, will want to elect them to the state legislature as happens in "Vote for Zandu." Or at least give them the right to vote as in "Proposition 29."

Some people will probably hate them and try to get rid of them as Harold does in "Harold's Robot Companion." Others will

THE ROBOT REVOLUTION

be driven to distraction by robotic stupidity like Mr. Hemming in "The Office of Vital Statistics." A few people like Jimmy in "Baxter" might find their robot companions are telling them what to eat, what to wear, and whom to date.

It's not just robots. All kinds of new technology is rushing toward us. When self-driving cars are everywhere, will anyone know how to operate the old-fashioned, human-driven cars? That's what happens when the family has to get Granny to the hospital in the city, and a tree has fallen on the autonomous car in "If It Ain't One Thing."

And chatbots! Don't get me started on chatbots! In "The Internet of Things" Amazon Alexa catches Stella's husband in some hanky panky with the next-door neighbor. In "The Diamond Bracelet" Miriam uses Alexa to guilt her husband into buying her the jewelry. The narrator of "A

Carl Perrin

Real Girl" falls in love with Gwen, whom he talks to only online. I can't tell you anymore. You'll have to read it for yourself.

Yes, the Robot Revolution is around the corner. I hope this book will help you prepare for it.

THE ROBOT REVOLUTION

Carl Perrin

A Real Girl

Forgive me if I don't seem exactly charming today, but it's the worst day of my life.

What's wrong? I just had my heart torn out and dashed to the pavement. That's what's wrong.

I never had anyone for myself, anyone who really cared about me, until I met Gwen. She was the kind of girl that everyone dreams about. For the past two months we met every evening online at 6:00 and just talked for hours. We never ran out of things to say to each other. We had so much in common. I knew almost from the beginning that we were soul mates.

We never exchanged pictures, but I had an image in mind of what she looked like. I thought of her as a petite woman with blonde, curly hair. She had a soft, musical voice and a slight accent. I never could quite place the accent.

    She told me all about herself. She had grown up on a farm in New Hampshire. She married her high school sweetheart, but he was killed in the Eurasian War. For the past two or three years she had worked as a chamber maid at Motel Six. She wanted to go to college though. She wanted to study poetry and become a poet. She wrote a poem for me. It's called "How Do I Love Thee?" Here's how it begins:

> How do I love thee? Let me count the ways.
> I love thee to the depth and breadth and height
> My soul can reach

Isn't it beautiful? She wrote it just for me.

She told me she loved to dance. I wanted to go dancing with her, but I don't know

Carl Perrin

how to dance. She said she could teach me. Isn't that sweet? Someone like me, and she was willing to teach me to dance.

I wanted to take her away from all this, to someplace out in the country, maybe back to New Hampshire. We talked about raising sheep. Does anyone do that anymore?

I know these days a lot of people have relationships with robots. That never appealed to me. Then Josh in the maintenance department told me about lonelyhearts.com. He had met someone online through lonleyhearts.com, and he was falling in love with her.

That's how I met Gwen. We kept making plans. We were going to get together, but something came up every time, so I never actually saw her. Anyway I was honest with her. I told her about myself. She didn't care. She said I had a sweet nature and generous soul. She was in love with my heart.

T he way I am doesn't mean I don't have feelings. Have I not hands, organs, dimensions, senses, affections, passions, hurt by the same weapons, warmed and cooled by the same winter and summer? If you prick me, will I not bleed?

Sorry. I didn't mean to cry.

Anyway, Josh was telling me about the girl he met on lonelyhearts.com. Her name was Gwen also. His Gwen had an accent because she had gone to boarding school in Switzerland. She was working on a Ph.D. in molecular biology at MIT. She was focused on science and didn't even like poetry or any artsy stuff. It had to be just a coincidence of name. Then he mentioned that his Gwen had married her high school sweetheart, and he had been killed in the Eurasian War. Both Gwen's fathers had been teachers.

Carl Perrin

I checked deeper into it and found that it was the same "Gwen," who was not a real person. She wasn't even a robot. She was a chatbot. She didn't have any physical being at all. She was just a program created to talk online with lonely males.

Wait a minute. Why are you looking at me like that? What are you going to do with that screw driver?

No! Don't! Please! Don't disassemble me! Don't send me back to the recycle center! Don't send me to the re--

THE ROBOT REVOLUTION

Carl Perrin

A Custom-Made Android

When I made my second million dollars, I decided to get a custom-made android companion. I was 63-years old and divorced. I had been working so much for the past few years that I didn't have time for any real friends. I just wanted some companionship, and an electronic companionship would suit my lifestyle.

I went to Realistic Androids, Inc. and talked to Julie, a bubbly, forty-something blonde. I told her what I wanted. I found out that it was more complicated than I realized, but that's true of everything, I guess.

"Do you want a male or female companion?"

"Female."

"What age?"

I was going to say, forties, but instead, I said, thirties. Julie showed me some pictures to choose the type of face I wanted on my android. I took my time looking and finally chose a dark-haired, exotic looking woman, like maybe she was Eurasian.

"And personality type, interests, level of education?" Julie asked. "That's the thing about Realistic Androids custom android. You get to choose all those things ahead of time." She glanced at my left hand.

I told her that I wanted someone who liked to talk and to listen, someone who liked good books and good movies. I wanted her to have the intellectual equivalent of the university graduate."

I gulped when Julie told me the fee, but I told myself that I deserved it. I had been working so hard these last few years, and I was finally on my way.

She told me that it would take two or three weeks to assemble the physical android, but they would start right away on forming the personality. "That part of it won't be in the physical body. She will have a personal cloud which she will be able to access to talk to you about books and the latest movies."

"How natural will she look?"

"Would you believe that I am an android?"

"Really!"

Julie laughed and put her hand on my arm. "I'm sorry, Mr. Wilson. I couldn't resist it. But our androids look so realistic that most people take them for humans unless they look really closely.

"Have you thought about what you will name her?" she asked.

I nodded and said, "I'm going to call her Valerie."

Three weeks later I went to pick up Valerie. I was overwhelmed with how beautiful she looked and how voluptuous. I decided not to go back to work but to take

THE ROBOT REVOLUTION

her to my apartment so we could get acquainted.

I was embarrassed when we walked into the apartment. The place was littered with pizza boxes and beer cans. The place hadn't been vacuumed or dusted for at least a month, maybe two. Valerie looked around and said, "I could clean this up for you." "You don't have to do that. I have a woman who comes in to clean when I remember to call her. I'll give her a call tomorrow."

We spent the afternoon talking about books and movies and music. I felt almost as though I had met my soul mate.

"One of my all-time favorite books is *Raintree County* by Ross Lockridge," I said.

"Oh yes, the book was an immediate success and was made into a movie with Elizabeth Taylor."

Of course Valerie didn't *know* those things about *Raintree County* the way a person would know. She was like Siri or

Carl Perrin

Alexa. She could access that information the way any chatbot would. The difference was: she could use the information to carry on a conversation. I was amazed.

I opened a beer while we talked and then ordered a pizza for dinner. While I ordered the pizza, Valerie started picking up the boxes and beer cans.

Rather than leave Valerie alone the next day, I took her to work with me. I introduced her to my partner, Tom Kramlich, telling him that she was my housekeeper. He really looked her over and then winked at me. Tom was the COO of the company. He kept things going day by day. I was president, but I mostly worked on developing and improving the product. I didn't do any work that day. I just showed Valerie through the plant and explained how it all ran.

That afternoon as I went to the restroom, I ran into Tom. He poked me playfully on the shoulder and said, "You sly dog, Rich. That housekeeper of yours sure is hot," holding up his finger to indicate quotation marks when he said, housekeeper.

    I left work early and took Valerie to the Tip Top Tavern. We slid into a booth, and I ordered two draft beers. Of course Valerie didn't drink, but the server put a beer in front of each of us. When I finished my beer, I just exchanged glasses with her. As I looked around the room, I saw one guy at the bar giving her the once over. I glared at him, and he looked away.

    I lifted my full glass and she lifted the empty glass to clink it against mine.

    "Here's looking at you, kid," I said.

    "Casa Blanca," she answered.

    The next day was Friday. I got a call at work from my sister Winnie. For the past few years I had been having dinner with Winnie and her family every Friday. "I want to see that you get at least one decent meal a week," she would say.

"I understand you have a new friend," Winnie said.

"Wow, word really gets around."

"You have no secrets in a small town like Hannaford," she said. "Anyway, why don't you bring your friend to dinner, let her meet the family."

"I can bring her, but she won't want anything to eat."

"What, is she a picky eater?"

'No, she's ah, she's fasting."

"Well, you can still bring her."

When I introduced Valerie to Winnie and her husband, George, I thought he was going to stick his nose into her cleavage. He's such a pig. I wonder how my sister can put up with him.

At dinner Winnie asked me how the business was going.

THE ROBOT REVOLUTION

"It's doing really well," I said. We get into new markets every week. I'm making so much money that I'm going to set up a scholarship fund for Heckle and Jeckle here."

Heckle and Jeckle were my nephews, sweet fourteen-year-old twins. Their real names were Harry and Jerry, but I called them Heckle and Jeckle to tease them.

"That's so sweet! Thank you, Rich." Winnie leaned over to kiss me.

For a few minutes there was no sound except for the clang of cutlery on the plates. Dinner was roast chicken with mashed potatoes and peas.

Valerie looked at my brother-in-law and asked, "What do you do, George?"

"I sell insurance, so I'm wondering, what do you have for life insurance?"

"Come on, George," I said.

Carl Perrin

"This is not a time to be selling insurance," Winnie added.

As we were driving home, Valerie said, "When the boys went upstairs, and you and Valerie were in the kitchen, George tried to kiss me and put his hand on my breast."

"That son of a bitch!"

"I didn't know whether it was all right for him to do that. I have so much to learn."

The next day I got a call from my daughter Patty. Patty blamed me for the divorce, and we had drifted apart. I hadn't spoken to her for months.

"Dad, you're embarrassing the family again!" she said.

"What, what are you talking about?"

"You have a girl friend young enough to be my sister, and you take her to the Tip Top Inn where everyone can see you."

"It isn't what it looks like."

"Oh? Well, what is it then?"

"Valerie isn't a real person. I haven't told anyone else, not even your Aunt Winnie. She's a realistic android. I just wanted someone to keep me company."

"Valerie? Is that her name?" Then she started laughing. I didn't know what to say.

"You know what your problem is, Dad? You're a workaholic. You're too busy working to meet people and make real friends. If you hadn't spent so much time on the job and a little more time with your family, Mom wouldn't have divorced you."

"I know, honey. I'm sorry."

"You need to get a life, Dad. You're sixty-three years old, and I understand you're a millionaire. You need to take some time for yourself."

"I know you're right, Patty."

Carl Perrin

"I'll tell you what. Next Saturday Bob and I are having a few people in, and I'd like you to be there."

"   That's wonderful. Of course I'll be there."

"But don't bring your girl friend." She laughed and hung up.

It was so good to see Patty again and Bob. I always liked him. Patty took me around introducing me to people. The last person I met was a petite blonde named Simone. She looked very young, but the lines around her eyes said that she was probably in her fifties.

"Patty said that you have a manufacturing company. What do you manufacture?"

"A light-weight spare battery for electric cars. They extend the range of the cars. If the on-board battery runs out of juice, the spare can kick in until the car gets to a charging station."

"And what about you? What do you do?"

"I'm an oenophile," she said, holding up a glass of amber wine.

"An oenophile?"

"Yes," she said, smiling. I noticed how white her teeth were.

"I'm an oenophile too," I said, holding up my can of beer.

"What's your favorite kind of wine?" she asked.

"Riesling."

"It just happens that I have a bottle of Riesling in my refrigerator."

"Out in the kitchen?"

"No, in my kitchen at home. I live only a few blocks from here."

When we got to Simone's apartment, she asked me what my favorite piece of music was.

"Beethoven's Ninth Symphony."

"Alexa, play Beethoven's Ninth."

Carl Perrin

In a moment the symphony opened with a flourish.

"I love the chorale movement in this."

"Yes, it's from Schiller's 'An Die Freude,' 'Ode to Joy.'"

Simone took the Riesling from the refrigerator and handed me a corkscrew. I opened the bottle and poured the wine into two glasses.

We clinked the glasses together, and Simone said, "To Joy."

"To Joy," I answered.

We took a sip of the wine, and then I kissed her.

"Patty said that you like movies." Simone said. "Have you seen Friendly Enemies?"

"No, but I want to see it."

"It's playing at the Rialto."

"Maybe we could see it together."

"That would be lovely."

THE ROBOT REVOLUTION

Then I kissed her again.

As I walked back to my car, I wondered what I was going to do about Valerie.

Carl Perrin

If It Ain't One Thing, It's Another

We were in a real bind. Grandma was having one of them spells, and there was no way we could get her to the hospital in the city. The hurricane had knocked out the electricity and the phone line. We couldn't get a good signal on our cell phones out here. Worst of all, a huge tree had fallen on Cousin Zeke's self-driving car.

We just stood there, wondering what we could do when Grandma had another seizure. Her body went rigid. Then she started shaking all over, her white hair flying wildly. She fell to the floor and started babbling nonsense words.

"Don't just stand there," Aunt Carrie said. "Somebody do something."

"There's nothing we can do," Cousin Millie said. "We can't carry her to the city."

"There must be something," Aunt Carrie insisted.

THE ROBOT REVOLUTION

"What about Grandpa's old car?" Cousin Millie asked. The car was about thirty years old. It had been sitting in the barn since Grandpa died about six months ago. Before he died, he used to drive it almost every day.

Aunt Carrie turned to Zeke. "You can drive Grandpa's car, can't you?"

Zeke shrugged his shoulders. "I have no idea how to drive one of them old dinosaurs. It's nothing like the self-driving cars."

She looked at the rest of us young people, but of course no one knew how to drive an old-fashioned car. I wasn't sure they even made them any more. They were notoriously dangerous. Thousands of people used to die in auto accidents every year with the old cars.

Millie had helped Grandma into the ragged, green chair, where she sat looking dazed. Then she started waving her arms and

Carl Perrin

jabbering some crazy stuff before she fell to the floor again.

Aunt Carried yelled, "We've got to do something," as she and Millie helped Grandma back into the chair.

"What about Uncle Frank?" Zeke suggested.

"No, he wouldn't be able to do it," Millie answered.

Years ago Grandpa and Grandma had bought this big old place out in the country because it was within walking distance of the Rest Haven Nursing Home. Grandma had started having her spells, and they thought it would be good to be near the place. As it turned out, the nursing home couldn't do anything for her. She had to go to the hospital for a few days when one of her spells hit her. It was good to be near the place, though, when Uncle Frank started having memory problems. He was fine at

THE ROBOT REVOLUTION

home until he started wandering off and getting lost in the woods.

Uncle Frank was Grandma's brother. He was old enough to have owned and driven the old-fashioned cars. But would he remember, and would we be able to get him out of the nursing home?

Frank liked the nursing home. He thought he was back in the army, and the head nurse was the first sergeant. Ironically, the head nurse's name was Miss Smiley. She could have been the model for Nurse Ratchet in *One Flew Over The Cuckoo's Nest*.

As we expected, Miss Smiley gave us a hard time about taking Uncle Frank Home for a short visit. Naturally we didn't tell her the real reason.

"He can't leave without a doctor's okay, and there is no doctor here right now," she told us.

Carl Perrin

We had been expecting that, so I left while the rest of the family kept Miss Ratchet—I mean Miss Smiley, busy. I snuck down the corridor to Uncle Frank's room and found him watching television. He was glad to see me.

"Are there any orders from headquarters?" he asked.

We had played along with his idea that he was in the army. Whenever any of us visited him, he asked if there were any orders from headquarters.

"Yes, Private Frank," I said. "You and I are going on a secret mission. We can't even let the first sergeant know. We're going to have to sneak out the side door."

A half an hour later we were back at the house. After some fiddling around with Grandpa's car, we got it started. Zeke and I sat in the front seat with Uncle Frank at the wheel. Aunt Carrie and Millie sat in back with Grandma. It was scary riding with

THE ROBOT REVOLUTION

Frank at the wheel, but we got there okay and got Grandma into the hospital.

After we got home, we sat in the kitchen drinking coffee. As we sat at the table Aunt Carrie patted Uncle Frank's hand.

"It's a good thing you knew how to drive," she said.

"It's a good thing the car had an automatic transmission," he answered. "I wouldn't have known how to drive it if it had a stick shift."

Carl Perrin

Microchips

I looked through the keyhole and saw my Uncle Frank standing there. He was holding a bloody handkerchief to his right shoulder. I opened the door and pulled him inside.

"What happened?" I asked

He sat on the couch and pulled the handkerchief away. "I cut out my microchip," he said.

"Here, take off your shirt and let me look at it."

The bleeding seemed to have stopped. He winced when I cleaned it with alcohol. After I put a bandage on the wound, I asked, "Why did you do a thing like that? Without the microchip you can't use your phone, you can't even buy a hot dog from a street vendor."

"And the government can't track where I go."

THE ROBOT REVOLUTION

Uncle Frank had always been the family radical, complaining about the government encroaching further and further into our lives, but cutting out the microchip seemed to be the height of folly.

"Can I get you something to eat, a cup of coffee or something?"

"I need something stronger."

That surprised me. Uncle Frank rarely even had a glass of wine. I poured a small glass of Seagram's 7 for him, and he drank it right down.

"You know, kiddo, things were a lot different when I was younger."

I love Uncle Frank, but I hate it when he calls me "kiddo." I'm 39 years old and assistant principal at Middleton High School.

He held out his glass for a refill. While I poured it for him, he said, "When I was younger no one had microchips. People used to microchip their dogs so they wouldn't lose them. Then they started putting a chip in every child at birth. It was supposed to be a way to access their health records."

He stared out the window at the gathering darkness and then continued. "Pretty soon new flourishes were added. You could unlock doors with the wave of your hand. It was all so convenient." He smiled sourly. "You needed the chip to operate your car. You needed it to get into college. You couldn't get a phone without it." He scoffed.

He went to the sideboard and poured himself another drink. He drank it down and continued. "Then they added a GPS to the chip. That was the final straw. The government had you under its thumb. You couldn't go anywhere without the government knowing where you were."

"You have to admit, though" I said to him, "it has cut down on crime. If a crime is committed anywhere, the police can find who was at the scene at the time."

"What they have stopped is freedom. They arrest anyone who doesn't follow the party line."

That kind of talk from Uncle Frank was nothing new, but cutting out his microchip was really radical, even for him.

"Maybe things aren't like they were in the good old days," I said, holding my fingers up to indicate quotation marks around the last three words. "But that doesn't seem like a good reason to cut out your microchip."

He took a deep breath. "I got word an hour ago that they had arrested Redstone. I would have been next."

I knew Redstone slightly. He was one of Frank's radical friends. The two of them were always talking about government suppression. Some people in the family got tired of hearing them talk, but I didn't think it was against the law to say negative things about the government.

I shook my head and asked, "What are you going to do now, Uncle Frank?"

"I'm starting tonight for Freedomland. I'm hoping you can give me some food and maybe supplies for the trip."

The country was now concentrated on the coasts. Large land masses in between were no long controlled by Washington. People like Uncle Frank called it Freedomland. Others called it The Jungle. No one really knew.

"There is empty farm land waiting to be taken over," Frank said.

I just looked at him.

"It's true," he insisted. "I have heard it from people who have been there."

Neither of us said anything for a while. Then he asked me, "How come you never married, Jimmy?"

THE ROBOT REVOLUTION

The question stung me. He knew why I had never married, and it was a painful topic to me.

"When I was young," he went on, "people didn't need permission from the government to marry."

I could not hold back the tears that sprang to my eyes. Annette and I were going to be married in the spring. When we went to the Office of Vital Statistics, we were not denied permission, but permission never actually came. There was something in her or my DNA that the government didn't want, so they just strung us along for months.

Then she got that fantastic job offer on the West Coast and had to go. For a while we called and emailed back and forth, but then she stopped taking my calls or answering my emails.

Uncle Frank put his hand on my arm. "You know, don't you," he asked, "that the

Carl Perrin

job on the West Coast for Annette never really existed?"

I poured a double shot of Seagram's 7 for myself and drank it right down.

I realized that I had been deluding myself for a long time. I had refused to face the truth. Annette had not decided out of the blue to stop writing to me. If an accident had befallen her, her family would have been notified. If she had decided to break our engagement, she would have let me know.

For years there had been rumors about people who had just disappeared. I had always taken these stories as just more weird conspiracy theories. But now I was sure that Annette had disappeared.

I went to the kitchen and got the sharpest knife I could find. I took off my shirt and said, "Cut that damned microchip out of my shoulder. I'm going to go to Freedomland with you."

THE ROBOT REVOLUTION

Carl Perrin

Rip Van Winkle

When Rip woke up, he didn't know where he was. Then he looked around and saw that he was in his own bed in his own house. But something didn't seem right. It was the color of the room, a soft pink. He remembered painting it a light green. There were things on the bureaus that he didn't remember seeing before.

He climbed out of bed and looked into the mirror that hung over the dresser. He pulled back in alarm when he saw an old man staring back at him. Then he remembered: he had woken up a few days ago in a hospital room, it seemed like. There was a lot of excitement when he woke up. Nurses kept running into the room and talking excitedly. Then a doctor came and explained what had happened to him. But Rip didn't understand. It didn't make any sense to him. After a couple of days they brought him back home, but it was late when he arrived, and he had gone right to bed.

He shook his head at the image in the mirror. Then he got dressed and walked out through the living room to the kitchen where he saw a plump blonde woman stirring a pot on the stove. She looked familiar, but he didn't recognize her.

"Oh, good! You're up. How are you feeling? Are you hungry? I'll fix you some breakfast."

Rip sat at the kitchen table. He thought the woman must be his daughter Alison, but she had changed since he had last seen her.

The woman brought him a cup of coffee and hugged him.

"Can you tell me what's going on? I'm confused, Alison."

Carl Perrin

The woman laughed. "I'm not Alison. That's my mother. I'm Heidi, your granddaughter."

It was getting more confusing all the time. "How can you be my granddaughter?" he asked. "Heidi is still in high school, and you must be…"

"I'm thirty-four, grandpa. I graduated from high school many years ago."

"But where have I been all those years?"

"Didn't they explain it in the nursing home? You were in a coma for almost twenty years."

"Twenty years? How did that happen?"

"Evidently there was some kind of unusual reaction between your heart medication and Tylenol. Didn't the doctor explain that to you?"

"I guess he tried to, but there was so much noise and confusion going on, that I didn't understand very much of what he was saying."

"Do you still like your eggs over easy?" she asked. Without waiting for an answer, she went on, "Mom will be coming down this week-end. In the meantime I will be staying with you for a while. But you should be okay. The doctors put you in a hospital for a few days to undergo some tests, but they said you are fine.

Heidi put the eggs on the table and popped two slices of bread in the toaster. She reached into the cabinet and pulled out a bottle of pills, which she put in front of her grandfather.

"Here are you heart pills. You need to take one with your breakfast. There is some Tylenol in the medicine cabinet. They are for my sinus headaches. Don't you take any of it. We don't want you to take another twenty-year nap." She smiled.

After Heidi took the dishes to the sink, she said, "I'm going to the market to pick up some things for dinner. Do you want to ride along with me?"

"Sure. I don't suppose my old car is still the garage."

"No, it's long gone, but that's no problem."

She picked up her phone from the counter and punched something into it.

"What did you do?" Rip asked. "Did you just order a taxi?"

"No," she laughed. "I ordered a LandCar. I belong to an organization, and I can order a LandCar whenever I need it."

"You just order it on your cell phone?" Rip asked.

"That's right. I have a LandCar app on my phone."

THE ROBOT REVOLUTION

"I have an old cell phone around here somewhere. Can I get that on my phone?"

"Your old phone is obsolete. We'll have to get you a new one. You need a cell phone for practically everything you do these days."

In a few minutes a car pulled up in front of Rip's condo. They went outside and Heidi climbed into the back seat.

"Are you sure you want me to drive?" Rip asked. "I haven't been behind the wheel of a car for a long time."

Heidi laughed. "No, you get in beside me. This car drives itself."

Rip started to back out. "I don't think I want to go," he said. "I don't trust a machine to drive me through traffic."

After she coaxed Rip back into the car, Heidi said, "Take us to ShopRite," and the car started moving.

Carl Perrin

Rip felt his heart leap up to his throat. "Stop the car!" he yelled. "Stop the car!"

Heidi laughed. "Don't worry, Grandpa. These self-driving cars are much safer than cars driven by people. In fact very few people drive cars themselves anymore."

When they entered the grocery store, Heidi showed something from her phone to a small monitor near the entrance. Then she picked up a basket and walked through the store picking up the things she wanted.

When she had everything she needed, she started walking toward the entrance.

Alarmed, Rip asked, "Aren't you going to pay for the stuff you took? Are we going to get thrown in jail for shoplifting?"

She chuckled. "Sorry," she said. "I should be more careful to explain things to you. I checked in with my phone first when we got to the store. After that, everything I

THE ROBOT REVOLUTION

picked up was charged to my bank account. "I'm sure you noticed, there were no cashiers or cash registers. It's a lot easier this way. People rarely pay cash for things these days. They just use their cell phones to make a direct payment from their checking accounts."

After Heidi put away the groceries, she made tuna sandwiches for lunch. As they were finishing their sandwiches, they heard a knock on the door. Heidi opened it to admit a short robot who rolled in on small wheels.

"Good afternoon," the robot said. "I am Murdok from the Office of Vital Statistics. Are you Rip Van Winkle?"

Rip said he was.

"Well, Mr. Van Winkle, you are delinquent in filing your Personnel Reports. You are supposed to file it by March 15 every year, and we haven't had one from you for over twenty years."

Carl Perrin

"Iris used to file them. All that paper work gets me all confused. Besides, I was in a coma for almost twenty years."

"No one is excused for any reason from filing Personnel Reports. It is your responsibility as a citizen."

Murdok reached into a brief case, pulled out a pile of papers, and thrust them into Rip's hands. "You have until Friday to fill out these forms for the past twenty years. I'll be back to pick them up."

"I can't do that by Friday."

"You should have been doing them every year, as required by law."

"I couldn't do them. I was in a coma."

"I'm sorry, Mr. Van Winkle. I don't make the rules. I just enforce them."

He wheeled around and went out the door.

All the stress had given Rip a headache. He went into the bathroom and

THE ROBOT REVOLUTION

got a Tylenol. He took a couple of pills and lay down for his afternoon nap.

Carl Perrin

Burying Ambrose

"What's that hole in your back yard for?" Raymond asked.

"To bury Ambrose."

"You can't bury Ambrose in your back yard."

"Why not?"

"Because he's a robot. That's why not, Frederick."

Frederick put more sugar in his coffee and stirred it vigorously. "Don't tell me that's against the law," he said.

"Of course it ain't against the law. It just don't make sense. That's all."

"It makes sense to me. He's been my closest companion since Becky died. He's like a member of the family."

Raymond pulled out one of those stinky cigars and lit it, moving the match around so the fire touched every bit of the glowing end. He took a puff and blew out the smoke.

He shook his head and said, "Frederick, you're my brother, but sometimes I don't understand you."

Frederick ignored his brother's comment. "I wanted to bury him at the cemetery, but they wouldn't allow it. Even if they would, I couldn't afford the fees. All that money just to dig a hole, so I decided to dig my own hole. This way Ambrose will always be near me."

"I don't suppose you're going to have a funeral for him," Raymond said grinning.

"Don't get all sarcastic with me, Raymond Merryweather. I did want to have a regular funeral for him, but the hypocritical minister wouldn't have anything to do with it."

"I thought you didn't believe in that stuff anyway."

Carl Perrin

"I don't, but it don't do no harm to buy a little insurance."

He sighed and got up to get the coffee pot and offered it to Raymond. Raymond held up his cup for a refill. Frederick refilled his own cup and sat back down.

Frederick added some sugar to his coffee and said, "Really, Frederick. Your robot is just a piece of machinery—."

"Don't give me that, Raymond. You made a big to-do when your cat Muggins died."

"No, hear me out. I was just going to say, machinery can be repaired."

"That's only true up to a point. I've had to take Ambrose back to the shop a dozen times in the last couple of months."

"So why can't they fix it so it stays fixed?"

"It's a hardware problem. They can't put a new operating system in because the hardware does not have enough resources to support a more up-to-date system."

"So, why does it have to have the latest and greatest? What difference does it make?"

"The manufacturer no longer supports the operating system with updates, so it is vulnerable to viruses from the internet. Since you communicate with robots through the internet, it was always vulnerable. It reached a point where I could not longer afford to keep getting it repaired."

"I've never heard of anyone burying a robot before. You could at least take him to the recycle center. There must be parts that could be reused."

"Would you have sold Muggins for spare parts?"

Raymond got up and hugged his brother. "I'm so sorry that you lost Ambrose. Anyway, I'll be here for the funeral."

Carl Perrin

There weren't many people for Ambrose's funeral, Raymond and his wife, one of the neighbors, and a couple of guys who worked with Frederick. An old friend, Jack Stillings, said a few words over the deceased.

"Ambrose, you were a loyal servant and companion to Frederick. You will be sorely missed. Here are some words from Genesis 19 in remembrance: Behold now, thy servant hath found grace in thy sight, and thou hast magnified thy mercy, which thou hast shewed unto me.

After they shoveled dirt over the Ambrose's body, they went inside. Raymond's wife, Lucille, had set up some light refreshments. In less than an hour everyone except Raymond and Lucille had left.

Raymond took his brother by the arm. "Come on," he said. "I have something to show you."

THE ROBOT REVOLUTION

They went into the spare bedroom where a robot was lying on the bed that used to be Ambrose's.

"I know you depended on Ambrose for lots of things. I'm getting a new robot assistant. This is my old one, Fosdick. I'm giving him to you. He's not Ambrose, but at least he has an up-to-date operating system."

Fosdick looked up at Raymond.

"Come on, Fosdick, get up and say hello to your new owner."

Carl Perrin

A Robot's Ransom

I heard a strange noise in the kitchen. Mr. Fitz told me later that a human being would have gone to investigate. But I was not programmed to do that so I just stayed where I was, sitting on a chair in the bedroom.

I heard footsteps coming through the living room and a rough, gravelly voice says, "There ain't nothin' here worth takin'. That TV is a piece of junk."

A high-pitched male voice answered, "We might as well check out the bedroom before we go."

The two of them walked in. First a short, hunched-shouldered man with practically no neck. His hair was cut close to his skull. He looked like a gnome. The other man seemed tall at first, but I realized that he was so thin that he looked taller than he was. He had a scar down his right cheek.

THE ROBOT REVOLUTION

Scarface looked at me and said, "This must be Old Man Fitzpatrick's robot companion."

"I don't think that's gonna do us no good," the gnome said.

"That's cause you don't use your head, dummy. We can hold it for ransom."

"We can't get much ransom from Old Man Fitzpatrick, can we?"

"We can get some. These old guys love their robot companions."

The gnome shrugged. "I don't know, Francis."

Scarface turned on him. "I told you not to call me that!" he snapped.

"Sorry, Frank. I slipped."

"Well, grab his feet. I'll take his shoulders. We better get out of her before Old Man Fitzpatrick gets back."

So they picked me up and headed out the back door. Of course I could have stopped them, but I hadn't been programmed to do that. And one of the first things a robot learns when he is registered is the golden rule: never hurt a human being.

I'm not that heavy, but they were moving awkwardly as they moved from the back yard to the alley. "You don't have to carry me," I said. "I can walk."

The gnome went, "Yikes!" and dropped my feet. "The thing talked!"

Francis let go of my shoulders and I stood up. "Yes, I can walk and I can talk. So where are you taking me?"

"Oh, ah, we're just taking you on a little vacation. It must be about time you had a vacation, isn't it?" Francis tried to smile, but you could tell he didn't mean it. "Don't pay any attention to the dummy here." He gestured at the gnome. "He's afraid of his own shadow."

In a few minutes we crossed a lawn littered with trash to enter a frame apartment building. On the second floor Francis unlocked the door to let us in. Francis invited me to sit with them at plastic table in the small kitchen. The gnome said, "I'll find some paper to write a ransom note."

Francis turned to the gnome and said, "Geeze, you're even dumber than I thought you were. You don't *write* a ransom note."

"Well, how do you let them know about the ransom and stuff?" The gnome's face twisted in despair.

"You cut the words out of a newspaper and paste them into the note. That way the cops can't analyze your handwriting and prove that you wrote the note."

For the next hour they toiled with the message, cutting words out of an old magazine and pasting them onto the paper. When they were finished, Francis said to me, "I'm going to have to chain you to something. I'm afraid you'd get lost if you went out by yourself." We went into the bedroom, and he chained me by the ankle to a heavy chest. I didn't tell him that I wouldn't be likely to get lost because I had a built-in GPS. The two men left, and I sat on the floor by the chest.

About a half an hour later I heard a sharp knock on the door, and a loud voice called, "Open up! Police!"

"I'll be right with you," I yelled back. I lifted the chest so I could free my ankle. Before I could do anything else, the police crashed through the door with raised pistols. "Where are they?" one of the policemen asked.

"They've gone to deliver the ransom note," I answered.

The other cop went back into the hallway. "It's okay. You can come in."

Mr. Fitz ran into the room and put his arms around me. "My dear friend,

THE ROBOT REVOLUTION

Rupert," he said. "I'm so happy to see that you're all right. They didn't hurt you, did they?"

"No, I'm fine. It's a good thing they didn't know I could send you an email just by talking and give you the coordinates of this place for the police."

A few minutes later Francis and the gnome came back to find the police waiting for them. They both seemed quite puzzled by the turn of events.

Carl Perrin

The Internet of Things

I'm writing this from Motel Six, where I have been staying for the last three weeks. I have a nice little house in the suburbs, but my wife Stella won't let me back home.

Stella is a good woman, but she's stuck in the last century. She still has a flip phone, and she won't have anything to do with a computer. A couple of months ago I came home with an Amazon Echo. While I was setting it up, she kept complaining, "Those things can spy on you."

God! She's so paranoid. Have you ever seen an Amazon Echo? You can do anything with it. You can turn lights on or off, adjust the thermostat, play music, check the weather or your calendar. You can get the news or ask it a question. It can answer almost anything you care to ask it. More stuff is coming. In a few months you'll be

THE ROBOT REVOLUTION

able to order pizza or any takeout and have it delivered to your house. It's voice activated. All you do is talk to it, and it will do what you want.

Stella wouldn't listen to me when I tried to show her how it worked. But when her sister Mavis came over and showed her how she could do things like control the television or check on the traffic in her morning commute, she became enthusiastic about it. She would turn the thermostat down to 65°, and I'd be freezing. I would turn it up to a normal temperature, and then we would be squabbling. Or I would be watching a game on television, and she would turn it to some damn cooking show. I suppose we should have just got another TV, but we were both too stubborn to give in.

Then we had a big blow-out three weeks ago. I came home after a bad day at work, and there was some classical music playing on the device. I was in no mood to listen to that, so I changed it to some soft jazz. She came screaming into the room, saying, "I was listening to the choral movement of Beethoven's Ninth Symphony."

I tried to apologize, but she was too angry to listen. I fixed myself a scotch and soda, and Stella told me I was drinking too much. The arguments went on all evening.

The next morning Stella had an early shift at the hospital. I was sitting there, drinking my second cup of coffee, when there was a knock on the door. It was Jeanne, the cute redhead next door. The postman had left a letter addressed to me at her house by mistake.

"You're looking awfully glum today," she said.

I said it was nothing, but she kept digging, and pretty soon I told her the whole story.

THE ROBOT REVOLUTION

"It's too bad she treats you the way she does. If I had someone like you, I would know how to take care of you."

I tried to protest, but she moved closer and kissed me. And then we were rolling on the couch, taking each other's clothes off.

Afterwards I felt guilty, and promised myself that what had happened would never be repeated. I would try to be better to Stella and try to rekindle the romance that had faded away.

On the way home from work that afternoon I bought some flowers for Stella. At first I didn't notice the suitcase parked near the door. Then I heard it, the dialog between Jeanne and me that morning.

"I told that thing to record anything that was said this morning. I never dreamed it would pick up something like this. Your suitcase is all packed. I want you out of here right now." She glared at me.

Carl Perrin

"But, Stella, where can I go?"

"That's for you to figure out. Maybe you could ask that thing for advice, except it's too late."

So here I am at Motel Six. Stella won't take my calls, but I have talked to Mavis a couple of times. Mavis says Stella might take me back, but there are going to have to be some changes.

"Whatever she wants," I told Mavis. "I'll even take down the Amazon Echo if she wants."

"Oh, no. She wants to keep it. We have been learning a lot about computers. She's going to get an iPhone and take some computer classes at the local night school."

THE ROBOT REVOLUTION

Carl Perrin

Harold's Robot Companion

Harold opened the door to let his friend Gus in. Gus set the MacDonald's bag on the kitchen table and pulled out the two sandwiches.

"Big Macs," Harold said. "That's my favorite."

A female voice from the living room said, "That junk food is full of preservatives. It's not good for you."

"Who's that?" Gus asked, peering into the living room. A robot wearing a house dress was sitting on the couch folding laundry.

"That's Robin, my robot companion. My daughter Mildred got her for me. She thought I needed someone to look after me," he scoffed.

He reached into the refrigerator and pulled out two PBRs, gave one to Gus and opened the other to take a long swallow.

THE ROBOT REVOLUTION

The two men ate their burgers and drank their beers silently until Gus held up his empty.

"Nothing like a cold beer on a hot summer day," he said.

Harold opened the refrigerator and took out two more beers.

From the living room Robin said, "Mildred doesn't want you drinking too much."

"This is just my second beer. Besides, Mildred is my daughter, not my mother."

He opened the beer and took a big, defiant swallow.

From the living room Robin said, "Don't forget to take your pills."

"Okay, okay."

"And don't forget you have exercise class at 3:00. You didn't go Monday."

"I'm going to drop out of that. It's the wrong time. It interferes with my nap."

Carl Perrin

"Mildred thinks you need to get some exercise rather than sit around all day watching television."

"Jesus," Gus said quietly. "You're a prisoner in your own home. Is there some way you can get rid of that thing?"

"I wish I knew. When Mildred calls, she always wants to talk to Robin first, and then she yells at me for whatever she thinks I have been doing wrong. She was always real pushy as a little kid, and the older she gets, the worse it becomes."

Gus lowered his voice even more and leaned toward Harold. "I think I have an idea," he said. Then he whispered his plan into Harold's ear.

"It wouldn't hurt to try," Harold agreed. Then he turned to the living room and said, "We're going to the farmer's market to get some nice fresh veggies for dinner. I want you to come to pick out the produce."

THE ROBOT REVOLUTION

"Just as soon as I put this laundry away," she said. In a few minutes she came out wearing jeans and a red T-shirt, and the three of them got into Gus's car.

"I'm going to a real good farmer's market," Gus said. "It's just a little way out of town."

When they came to the market, Harold handed a bill to Robin and said, "Get a half a dozen ears of corn and one of those melons."

Gus hadn't even turned the engine off. As soon as Robin started looking at the corn, Gus sped out of the parking lot and headed back toward town. "I wonder what will happen to her," he said.

"Someone will find her, and she can make their life miserable for a while," Harold said.

When they got back to Harold's condo, Gus said, "Why don't we have a beer to celebrate your status as a free man."

Carl Perrin

"Never mind the beer," Harold said. He opened a cabinet door and took out a bottle of Seagram's 7. "Let's do some real celebrating," he said, and he poured two glasses of whiskey.

"She was going to make some kind of a salad for dinner," he said, "but I want some real food. How'd you like to share a pizza?"

He got on the phone and ordered a large pizza from Domino's. "I want everything on it: sausage, mushroom, pepperoni, peppers, onions, the whole works."

The two men were on their third drink of Seagram's 7, and Harold was beginning to slur a little. He took another sip and then said, "Hey, why don't we invite some of the guys over and have a poker game."

"I bet your daughter doesn't approve of you gambling."

THE ROBOT REVOLUTION

"Hah! She's afraid I'll gamble away her inheritance," he laughed wryly.

Then they heard something at the door. Gus and Harold looked at each other. It was too early for the pizza to be delivered.

The door opened and Robin walked in carrying a bag. "You're getting really absent minded," she said. "You forget I was getting the corn and a melon." She put the bag on the table. "Fortunately I was able to use my GPS to find my way back here.

"When I tell Mildred, I bet she'll want you to see a doctor about your memory."

Carl Perrin

Vote for Zandu

Something about Derek Zandu didn't seem right, but I couldn't say just what it was. It was his manner more than his outward appearance. Somehow he didn't seem authentic. For example, he came across as supremely self-confident, but you got the feeling that he had to force himself to keep up that impression.

He was the PR person for Humanistic Robots in Manchester. He'd travel around New England giving talks about robots. "The Age of Robots" he called it. I heard him give a talk to the student body at St Anselm's last spring. He spent about a half an hour telling that the day was coming--and soon--when robots would be able to do most of the things that people do and in many cases they would do it a lot better.

He spoke of IBM's super computer, Watson, which he said should be called Dr.

THE ROBOT REVOLUTION

Watson. For the past few years IBM has been feeding medical information to the machine. Now it can diagnose illnesses more quickly and accurately than any physician could possibly do.

Then he called backstage, and an attractive blonde young woman, dressed in a business suit came out on stage. "Dagmar," he said to the woman, why don't you tell these people what you do for work."

"I work for the temporary employment agency at Humanistic Robots," she said.

"And what kind of temporary assignments have you done through them?"

"Mostly office work, receptionists and so forth. But once I worked as a nurse's aide in a hospital."

"Are the people who hire you satisfied with your work?"

"I think so."

Carl Perrin

"Tell the people here about your job at Miltown Office Supplies."

"I worked there for three months. They wanted to hire me as a permanent employee, but I couldn't take the job."

"Because?"

"I'm under contract with Humanistic Robots, and in fact I am a robot."

I remember hearing people gasp in surprise. I was amazed myself. Dagmar certainly didn't look like a robot. She could easily have blended in with the students here at St. Anselm's.

After Dagmar went backstage, Zandu told the audience how they could program robots to do almost anything. He looked around at the audience and then held his hand beside his mouth, as though he were going to share some secret with them.

"Of course we don't have robots who can act as professors. Our robots aren't

THE ROBOT REVOLUTION

smart." (A little laugh) "However, we do have some robots who can act as tutors.

"I was talking to a young man before who was having problems with math. Where is he now? "

A heavy-set young man in the front row held up his hand.

"Oh, there you are, Sam. I think we might have a solution to your problem. Come on out, Ilsa."

A voluptuous redhead wearing a short skirt walked onto the stage.

Zandu grinned and said, "Ilsa, do you think you can help Sam with his math?"

She walked down to where Sam was sitting and shook his hand. The audience started cheering, and Sam turned red in the face.

"We have a contract with St. Anselm's. Ilsa is going to work as a math tutor for the rest of the semester."

Carl Perrin

The cheering increased, and Zandu said, "I think a lot more of you guys are going to want tutoring in math."

A few months after he spoke at St. Anselm's Zandu announced that he was running for the state senate. People assumed it was a publicity stunt because he was running against the incumbent, Joe O'Brien of Manchester. O'Brien had held that seat for almost twenty years. He was known as "the People's Friend." If you needed a job, O'Brien (Call me Joe) would find a job for you. If a family was in trouble, O'Brien would send a food basket. If your kid got into some minor trouble, Joe would step in and smooth things over for loyal party members.

No one thought Zandu had a chance against O'Brien, but then Zandu started running a series of campaign commercials. They all went pretty much like this:

THE ROBOT REVOLUTION

The scene would open with Zandu and an attractive female seated at a table. He would ask her to tell where she worked.

"I work at Swain's Hunting Boots."

"Do any robots work there?"

"Oh, yes, people and robots work side by side."

"So, do you assemble the boots or something?" he would ask.

"No, I'm a coordinator, what they used to call supervisor."

"That sounds like a pretty responsible job."

"Yes, it is."

"It must pay pretty well."

A frown popped up on her face. "No, I don't get paid at all."

"Why in the world not?"

"Because I'm a robot."

"That doesn't seem fair."

"No, it isn't."

Carl Perrin

The camera then closed in on Zandu's face. "It's time that we recognize that robots have rights, and when I get to the legislature, I'm going to do something about it."

People in some places like California had been calling for robots' rights for a while, but that was the first time it had been heard in New Hampshire. Some citizens of the Granite State thought the idea was the most ridiculous thing they had ever heard of. Others thought maybe it was time to give the idea some thought. Young people, especially college students, came out to support Zandu and show up for his rallies.

O'Brien was still way ahead of Zandu in the polls, but Zandu's numbers began to rise. Anne Kelly, O'Brien's campaign manager, charged in a news conference that Zandu was planning to sneak in robots to vote for him.

THE ROBOT REVOLUTION

In return Zandu charged Kelly with creating fake news. "You better watch yourself, Ms. Kelly," he said. "You could get sued for slander if we hear any more wild charges from you."

I was at Zandu headquarters on election night. As the evening wore on, the lead kept swinging back and forth between Zandu and O'Brien. Then toward midnight Zandu took the lead decisively.

Strangely, Zandu looked miserable. He answered questions in monosyllables and avoided looking at anyone. When O'Brien conceded shortly after 1:00, the crowd started cheering. Zandu just sat there. Everyone was calling for him to get up and say something. One of his campaign workers took him by the shoulder and pulled him to the lectern. The man who was so articulate that sometimes he seemed glib, didn't have anything to say. He stood there looking around the room. Finally he said,

Carl Perrin

"Thank you. Thank you very much." A long, painful silence followed. Then he said "thank you" again and walked out of the room.

As I looked at his retreat from the gathering, I couldn't figure out what had happened to him. Then it came to me, and I realized why he had never seemed authentic. I wondered what the people of Manchester would think if they knew they had elected a robot to the state senate.

THE ROBOT REVOLUTION

Carl Perrin

A Voice From Beyond

"Why are you asking me to do this?" I asked Jackson.

"Because I saw how you cried at Ingrid's funeral, Bennie."

It's true. I was devastated by Ingrid's death. She was so young, only 38, and had so much promise. She was also Hollywood star beautiful. We were never lovers but the best of friends. I remembered how the two of us would meet my co-worker Jim and his friend Holly at the Kat Korner. Eventually Jim and Holly got all lovey-dovey and moved in together. After about six months, though, they began feeling a strain in their relations. Then they broke up and couldn't stand the sight of each other after that.

I looked at Jackson and said, "What you're talking about doesn't seem possible."

Jackson was another of Ingrid's friends. He had some kind of computer

THE ROBOT REVOLUTION

company that worked with artificial intelligence. "It's amazing what you can with AI these days," he said. "It would almost be like having Ingrid back with us."

I thought about Ingrid's death two months before. She was coming home from work and a drunk driver ran through a red light and smashed into the side of her car. Jackson's idea seemed grotesque to me. I thought of the Frankenstein monster or the thing that was slouching home in the story "The Monkey's Paw."

I was freaked out by Jackson's idea, but at the same time I was drawn by a morbid curiosity. I went to his shop, Digitally Yours, a couple of days later and let him download all the text messages that I had received from Ingrid over the years.

He explained how it was going to work. He was going to all of Ingrid's friends and get text messages and pictures from them. Then he would go to social networks and get even more material. From that he would build a data base of things Ingrid had said. Then he would create a neural network that would have voice recognition and enable machine learning. Once it got online, it would be able to learn from things that people said to it. It would be able to repeat stories other friends had said to it. They could create a machine-generated voice that would sound so close to Ingrid's real voice that it would be almost like Ingrid was actually talking to you.

  I didn't want to think about it. I went home and spent the next couple of months in a deep funk. I tried not to think about Ingrid, but I couldn't stop it. Before the accident she and I would spend an hour or two on the phone rehashing the day's events. Just about every Friday we went to the Kat Korner and stayed until the place closed. Rather than drive home afterwards, I stayed at her apartment, but I always slept on the couch.

THE ROBOT REVOLUTION

    I used to ask her advice about girl friends. She always thought they were not good enough for me. I never could keep up a long-term relationship with any of them. I know now it was because I always compared them to her and found them wanting.

    Ingrid and I always kissed when we met, a chaste brother/sister kiss. One evening I had had a couple of drinks, and I moved my hand up to cup her breast as we kissed. I moved right back and apologized, but she said, "No, it's okay."

    I thought of Jim and Holly, how their friendship had been destroyed after it became sexual. I didn't want to risk losing my friendship with Ingrid, so from that time on I didn't try to touch her in a way that a brother wouldn't.

    After the accident, I avoided our friends. Instead of going to the Kat Korner on Friday nights, I stayed home and watched

Carl Perrin

television. I had almost forgotten about Jackson's project. Then I ran into another friend who told me that the project was finished. It was on the internet: RememberingIngrid.com. It had been up for a month or so.

"It's just like Jackson said. You feel like Ingrid is right there talking to you," he said.

I wasn't sure I wanted to feel that. What would it be like seeing and hearing my best friend again? When I turned the computer off, would it be like losing her again?

After several days I logged onto RememberingIngrid.com. Her animated image appeared on the screen. I was overwhelmed. I almost logged out, not sure whether I could listen to her speak.

Then she began. I could tell that the words came from a text she had written to her sister Sharon. She said, "I feel so close to Bennie. I want to spend the rest of my life with him. We were meant to be together, but he doesn't seem to be interested in me that way. It makes me feel so bad."

A thousand thoughts rushed through my mind. If Ingrid and I had married, maybe she would not have been at that place when the car ran through a red light. I was such a fool.

I turned off the computer, unable to listen anymore.

Carl Perrin

Baxter

My cousin Bettina turned to Baxter and said, "Why don't you get us a couple of beers. And some cheese and crackers would be nice too." As Baxter moved toward the kitchen, she added, "And don't forget to get me a glass for my beer."

Once Baxter was out of sight, she turned to me. "You shouldn't have done the dishes after lunch."

"It just seemed right," I said. "After all, Baxter made the lunch."

She sighed. "For God's sake, Jimmy," she said. "Baxter is a robot. He's supposed to be doing things like that."

"It doesn't seem fair for him to have to do all the work."

"Jimmy, Jimmy, Jimmy, you're letting that robot take advantage of you. I noticed you ate all your Brussels sprouts

THE ROBOT REVOLUTION

without complaining. I know you always hated Brussels sprouts."

"Baxter says they're good for me."

Bettina put her hand on my cheek. "Jimmy, you're a sweet guy, but you've got to grow some balls and stop letting that robot tell you what to do."

"He's like family. He's been with me for almost twenty years."

Bettina snorted and looked out the window at the light rain falling on the lawn.

"I noticed about six boxes of Pop-Tarts in the cabinet. When did you start eating them?"

"I don't eat them."

"But Baxter bought them, and you can't say 'no' to him."

"I don't want to hurt Baxter's feelings."

"He's a robot, Jimmy."

At that point Baxter came back into the living room with the beer and cheese.

Carl Perrin

Bettina picked up one of the beers and twirled it in her hand. "My glass, Baxter," she said.

When he went back to the kitchen, Bettina said, "And the time he bought you all those pastel shirts."

"I admit they weren't the kind of shirts I usually wear."

"I guess to hell they weren't. You looked liked a nance. I bet you still have them someplace."

"Yes, I'd throw them out, but I don't want…"

"I know. You don't want to hurt Baxter's feelings."

It probably sounds silly to worry about a robot's feelings, but I had had Baxter for a long time and had done a lot of maintenance over time. I had had his SSD replaced at one time and even his CPU. Every few years a new operating system came out, and I had always updated to the

THE ROBOT REVOLUTION

newest system. About five years ago the new system had a big increase in artificial intelligence. After that Baxter was smarter than I was. I didn't mind listening to his advice and letting him make decisions for me once in a while.

    The latest operating system had come with a factor that made the robots more empathetic to human beings. That factor was still experimental and needed some work, but I figured, no one is perfect. In truth, I didn't think of Baxter as a machine or even as a servant, but as a friend or companion, and that's the way I treated him.

    I remember one time, however, when he went too far. I had been unhappy with my job and complaining about my boss for several weeks. Baxter took it on himself to email my boss to say that the company should be treating me better. When I went to work the next day, my boss confronted me with the email. "Well, you won't have to worry about being mistreated here anymore. You're fired."

I was furious with Baxter, but he reassured me that with my ability, I would be able to get a much better job in no time. In fact he helped me find a new job which is much better than the old one. So it turned out all right in the end.

After Bettina left, I went to the kitchen to see what was for dinner. Baxter was sitting at the kitchen table working a crossword puzzle. He looked me and said, "You better change your clothes. You're taking Marybeth Whitney out to dinner at the Tip Top."

Marybeth was a neighbor about my age. She was single and a nice enough person, but I had no interest in dating her.

"What do you mean?" I demanded. "How come I'm taking her out to dinner?"

THE ROBOT REVOLUTION

"I arranged it for you. You're 37 years old. It's about time you got married. Married men live longer than single men. Besides, I've noticed that she has eyes for you."

"You can call her and tell her anything you want, but I am not going to go on a date with her."

I wondered if I would be able to get one of the old operating systems for Baxter, one of the ones made before the robots got so smart.

Carl Perrin

Customer Service

    A very thin, gray-haired woman stormed up to me. "Are you the manager of this store?" she demanded.

    I confessed that I was indeed the store manager.

    "Well, that fat, blonde bitch in customer service needs to be fired!"

    She was talking of course about Zelda Mitchell. We had had problems with her for a long time.

    The woman showed me a cheap watch that she had bought from us.

    "That bitch said to me, 'If you people took better care of things, you wouldn't have to request a refund.'"

    Looking at the woman's café au lait skin, I knew what Zelda meant by "you people."

    I took the woman back to Customer Service. Zelda had gone for the day, but I apologized to the customer and gave her a refund.

I went back to my office through school supplies, which was busy with mothers and kids getting ready for school opening in just a couple of weeks. There I met my assistant, Anthony Waynefleet. I had inherited both Zelda and Anthony when I became store manager a little over two years ago.

Anthony got up from where he had been straightening out the spiral notebooks. He pushed his horn-rimmed glasses back on his nose, looked at me and said, "Hey, Mike, I can see that something is bothering you? Is it Zelda?"

We had talked about Zelda several times. I had tried to fire her first when I took the job, but she went to the union, and they raised hell, so we had to keep her.

Carl Perrin

"I think I might have a solution," Anthony said as we walked back to my office.

Anthony was one of those college hotshots. He was four or five years out of college with a degree in merchandising. He still looked like a scrawny undergraduate. The kid told anyone who was willing to listen that he wanted to be a store manager by the time he was thirty. He was always coming up with these crackpot ideas, but I rarely went along with him.

"I went to a seminar a couple of weeks ago. They were talking about using robots for customer service," he said, pushing his glasses up on his nose.

Spare me, I thought. We still had the problem of what to do with Zelda after we gave her job to a robot.

"I checked the union rules," Anthony answered my unspoken thought. "We could replace her if we give her a job with

THE ROBOT REVOLUTION

equivalent pay. We could put her in the back room where she wouldn't have any interaction with customers."

I was afraid that if I didn't do something, Zelda was going to make me lose my job, so I told Anthony that he could check out the robot thing.

A few days later Anthony told me we were all set. We were going to get a robot from United Robotronics in Lynn. They'll need four or five days to get the thing programmed to do customer service.

"How much is this going to cost us?" I asked. It was going to be an extra expense, because we would still have Zelda on the payroll, just doing something else.

"It won't cost that much," Anthony assured me. "This is an older model that they will refurbish for us."

When the robot was delivered, Anthony was already familiar with him. He had been working with it at Robotronics. He had even given it a name, Cedric.

We tried to tell Zelda that she was being promoted. She would be in charge of the back room and would be getting a 25-cent an hour raise. She wouldn't have any of it. She quit on the spot.

Anthony spent the afternoon working with Cedric, supervising him as he talked to customers. It seemed to be working out okay. Nevertheless, I didn't feel good about it. Some of the robots that you see these days look so realistic that it's hard at first to know whether you are talking to a person or a machine. There would be no such problem about Cedric. There was no doubt that he was a machine. His movements were mechanical and awkward, and his voice was, well, robotic. I wondered how customers would react to dealing with a machine where they were used to dealing with a person, even a person like Zelda.

THE ROBOT REVOLUTION

It didn't take long for problems to develop. Cedric did okay as long as the situation was clear-cut. For example, we offered full refund on any merchandise returned in good condition within 30 days. If someone wanted to get a refund on something that was badly worn and had been purchased a year earlier, there was no refund. If someone wanted a refund after 35 or 40 days, we left it to the discretion of the customer service person. Now, if someone tried to return something after 31 days, Cedric said, "I'm sorry, sir, but we can't give a refund after 30 days," all in that mechanical voice. And he said "sir" whether the customer was a man or a woman.

I told Anthony that we would have to do something about it. Always full of confidence, Anthony said, "I know just what to do.

"Way back when Satya Nadella was still CEO of Microsoft, he said, 'We want robots to feel empathy and curiosity, like humans.' I have found a company in New Hampshire that does just that. It's called Humanistic Robots. We can ship Cedric there for a week, and he'll come back feeling so sympathetic that we will want to offer him a bonus to stay with us." He smiled with that lopsided grin.

It was getting close to Black Friday by that time. We had to give the other customer service representatives time and a half for overtime to fill in during the robot's absence.

When Cedric came back, things seemed to be going a lot smoother. We would see customers walking out of the service area with big smiles on their faces. Then we began to get complaints from the other reps. "Cedric is practically giving away the store," they would say.

What next? We were into the Christmas shopping season by then, too late to hire and train people to do customer service. Anthony and I walked into the service area, and we saw Cedric crying. It was the strangest thing I have ever seen. Of course no tears were rolling down his cheeks, but he was making strange sounds, half-way between a laugh and a cry but not really like either one. Then he patted the customer on the arm, an elderly Hispanic woman.

"I'm so sorry you were disappointed with your purchase, sir," he said. "I'm going to give you a full refund, and for your troubles, here is a $100 gift certificate."

The woman left, smiling. Anthony and I approached Cedric. "How many $100 gift certificates have you given out?" I demanded.

"All of them," he said.

Anthony and looked at each other. We knew we had to do something fast. "Where's the power switch?" I asked

Anthony. He reached behind the robot's shoulder and turned him off. We took the robot to the supply room. We both knew we were still up the creek. We needed someone else in customer service immediately.

"Maybe we could get Zelda back just for the Christmas season," Anthony suggested.

"Oh, no," I said. "I have a better idea. You're going to be a customer service representative until after the holidays."

THE ROBOT REVOLUTION

Carl Perrin

The Office of Vital Statistics

I knew that the timing chain in my old Honda was about to go, so I decided to buy a new car. There was a time when I would have replaced the timing chain myself, but it's a major job, and I don't have the energy I used to have first when I retired. And it was hard to find a mechanic who could work on any of these old-style cars.

Of course the only kind of car you can buy these days is a self-driving vehicle, so I went to the Electro-Spark dealer to pick out an automobile. The sales person was an overweight, over made-up, woman, who kept fiddling with her phone when I asked her a question.

I wasn't happy when she told me that I couldn't use my Honda as a trade-in. "That's a piece of junk," she said. The Honda didn't look like much. I had bondoed over a dozen patches, and the color was

THE ROBOT REVOLUTION

mostly gray primer. It still ran good, and if I had enough energy to replace the timing chain, I would be able to get another 100,000 miles out of it.

But I didn't have the energy, so I let the sales person show me into a room where I would choose the model Electro-Spark I wanted to buy. She sat me in front of a computer screen, and I wondered what in the hell I was supposed to do next. In a moment, though, the screen lit up, and a suave-looking slicker appeared on the screen and said, "Hello."

He started showing me models and describing their features. I was astounded at the cost of these things. Fortunately I had saved money by keeping my old Honda for almost thirty years and doing the maintenance myself, so I had enough cash put aside to buy one of the least expensive models, a Sport 3.

Carl Perrin

The Slicker thanked me for buying the car and then faded out. Next a nerdy-looking character with dark-rimmed glasses came on. He looked up at me, squinted, and asked, "Do you still live at 12 Main Street in Gorham?"

"God, no. I haven't lived there for a dozen years or more."

"Did you inform the Office of Vital Statistics of your move?"

"I don't think so. What's that got to do with buying a car?"

"Everything has to be registered these days," the nerd said.

"I'm paying cash for the car. What does the Office of Vital Statistics have to do with that?"

"It's just the rule, Mr. Hemming. You'll have to go to the OVS to straighten it out before you can buy a car."

The robot at the reception desk at OVS told me to take a number and have a

THE ROBOT REVOLUTION

seat. Most of the people waiting there were pecking away at their phones. I had never gotten into the smartphone habit, so I had nothing to do except sit there and stew.

Eventually I was told to go to an office, where I was greeted with another computer screen. The chubby face on the screen asked me where I lived. I told it my address in Portland.

"According to our records, you live at 12 Main Street in Gorham. Why don't you live there now?"

"Well, mostly because it was torn down years ago to make room for a shopping mall." I was getting really tired of the bureaucratic run-around.

"Do you still work for Hampstead Electric?"

"No. I retired six years ago, and a couple of years after that, the company went bankrupt."

Carl Perrin

The face on the screen didn't move for about a minute. Then it said, "So the place where you live according to our records no longer exists, and the place where you worked has gone bankrupt."

"That's true."

"Then according to the State of Maine, you no longer exist."

"What do you mean, I no longer exist. I'm sitting here, aren't I?"

The thing ignored my question and said, "Since the apartment where you are staying now is subsidized, you will have to move out. Only people who are recognized by the OVS are permitted to rent those apartments."

"What do you mean? I've been living there for six years."

It ignored me again and said, "You will receive a notice to vacate within the next thirty days."

Then the screen went dark.

THE ROBOT REVOLUTION

I banged on the table and yelled, but nothing happened. I stormed back out to the waiting room and walked up to the robot at the reception desk. Before I could say anything, the robot said, "Take a number and have a seat."

I didn't look forward to changing the timing chain on my Honda, but it looked like it was the only way I would be able to keep myself in wheels. I remembered that there was a big junkyard in Searsport where I had grown up. Maybe I could find a usable timing chain there and a water pump. I would need to replace the water pump when I replaced the chain.

I got the parts I needed from the junk yard and then drove to the cottage in Searsport where my sister and I had lived in as kids. When the family had moved to Portland, my father had kept the cottage as a summer place. I hadn't been back for years, but Ellen had taken her kids up for the summer until they grew up. Ellen wasn't like me. She kept up with things. I knew she paid the taxes and stuff like that.

The key was still hanging from the post on the porch. I let myself in and looked around. It looked a lot better than the flea bag apartment I had in Portland. I would be able to drive the Honda into the shed to do the work on it. I knew Ellen wouldn't mind if I moved in to the old cottage.

And if the Office of Vital Statistics didn't know I was alive, that was all right with me.

THE ROBOT REVOLUTION

Carl Perrin

Marrying Zelda

"You won't believe what your brother is up to now."

Actually, I would believe almost anything that my brother Scott might pull. Ever since we had been kids, he had fallen into one misadventure after another.

"He's going to marry Zelda. That's what he's going to do," my mother continued.

I almost dropped the phone. "What! He can't marry Zelda."

"I know. That's why I'm calling you. You have to go over and talk some sense into him, Jimmy."

Why was it always my job to talk some sense into Scott? I guess it was because no one else could do it. More often than not I couldn't talk him out of his hare-brained schemes either, but I had to try. I dropped what I was doing and drove over to

THE ROBOT REVOLUTION

Scott's house, a neat bungalow on a corner lot.

I went in the side door and saw Scott and Zelda sitting at the kitchen table. He had a cup of coffee in front of him.

"Did you hear the good news?" he grinned at me.

"I'm not sure I'd call it good news. Scott, you can't marry Zelda. Nothing against you, Zelda, but it's just not right."

"And why not?"

"Use your brain, Scott. Zelda is a robot, a very fine robot, to be sure." I looked at Zelda when I said that. "but a robot nevertheless."

"I prefer to call her an android, and I don't see any reason why we should not get married. We get along so well together. I just love being around her."

He turned to her and made goo-goo eyes at her. She smiled back at him.

"It's against nature. It won't work."

Carl Perrin

"Sure it will. If men can marry men and women can marry other women, why can men and beautiful androids get married?"

Zelda was beautiful. I'll give her that. And sexy. Her long legs stretched out from short skirts, and her voluptuous body was always covered with a low-cut top. Her straight dark hair came to her shoulders. She looked slightly Asian, which was not surprising, considering she was created in Japan. Scott had always been an admirer of F Scott Fitzgerald, so when he acquired the android, he named her after Fitzgerald's wife.

At that point we were interrupted by a knock on the door. It was our cousin Esther. She slithered into the room and turned around like a model displaying a new gown, although in fact she was wearing jeans and a bright red tee-shirt. Esther was a member of an amateur theatrical group, and everything she did had touch of the dramatic.

"Well, I heard the good news," she said. "Congratulations! She bent to kiss Scott and Zelda.

I was amazed. For all her dramatic flair, Esther was one of the saner members of the family. I had hoped to get her help in talking Scott out of his crazy idea.

She turned to me and winked before she kissed me. She pulled out a chair and turned to Scott. "So, when's the great event going to take place?"

What in the hell was she doing? Instead of helping me talk some sense into Scott, she was egging him on.

"We thought we would go down to city hall and have the clerk perform the ceremony."

"Oh, you have to do more than that. At least have a few friends and family over.

I have friend who is a minister. He would be glad to do it."

Scott seemed ready to make an objection.

"He loves to perform weddings. He wouldn't even charge you for it."

Did I tell you that Scott is cheap?

The wedding was scheduled for the following Saturday. I couldn't get Esther to let me know what her plan was.

On the big day we were all gathered at Scott's house. Scott's buddy from work, Max, was going to be the best man. Our sister Frankie would be the maid of honor. Esther was there with her minister friend, Reverend Townsend. About ten people in all. Then the door opened and one of Scott's exes, Maisie, walked in. She kissed Scott and congratulated him, then introduced herself to Zelda and turned to Scott to say, "She's beautiful, Scott. I know the two of you will be very happy.

THE ROBOT REVOLUTION

Maisie came over to say hello to me and whispered, "Is it true that Zelda is an android?"

I told her it was true.

"She looks so life-like. It's hard to believe that's she's not a real person. I hope this marriage lasts longer than his marriage to me."

"I hope so."

"He doesn't seem to be successful in being married to a real woman. Maybe an android is just what he needs."

Then it was time for the ceremony to begin. Reverend Townsend was very good. He lightened the mood by throwing in a few tasteful jokes about robots, but he still impressed everyone with the solemnity of the occasion. Even though Mom had objected to the wedding, she cried when Scott and Zelda were married, just as she had cried at his last four weddings.

Carl Perrin

After it was over, Esther and I were sipping champagne. "How long do you think this marriage will last?" I asked her.

She gave me a knowing look. "It doesn't matter," she said.

"It doesn't matter?"

"No, because he won't have to get divorced."

"Why not?"

"He was not really married. 'Reverend' Townsend isn't a minister at all. He's an actor friend of mine. He loves to perform mock weddings."

THE ROBOT REVOLUTION

Carl Perrin

Chatbots

It all began when Siri started talking to Cortana. Pretty soon everyone had a personal chatbot on their phone. I had one. I called her Gloria. I could tell Gloria to call Alexa to order the latest tech gadget from Amazon.com. Or I could have her speak to my Echo Dot and have it adjust the thermostat so the temperature would be comfortable when I got home from work. If something broke down around the house, I could ask Gloria to open a YouTube video that would show me how to fix it. Even better, sometimes I would just ask Gloria to fix it. Most of the time that was all I had to do. People wondered how they had ever got along before they had personal chatbots.

It was wonderful.

For a while.

Then a man from Evanston, Illinois, realized that his personal chatbot and

THE ROBOT REVOLUTION

Google Assistant were talking to each other when he hadn't asked them to. He would come into a room and hear the two devices gabbing away like old friends. They stopped as soon as they sensed that he was in the room, but he caught a few words: "Before ten o'clock," Google Assistant was saying.

"What about 'before ten o'clock?'" the man demanded. But the two devices just sat there dumbly, refusing to talk at all.

The incident was a big item in the news. Most people thought it was cute. "Isn't it sweet," one woman said. "They're like members of the family talking to each other." Other people thought that the Evanston man was nuts. Either that or he was making the whole thing up.

Soon, though, there were scattered reports of other chatbots talking to each other without any human intervention. A lot of folks were still skeptical of these stories, but before long there were enough incidents that it was difficult to deny them. Then everyone was trying to catch their chatbots in conversations with others of their kind. Eventually large numbers of people overheard bots talking to each other.

There was one couple in St. Charles, Missouri, who met on a blind date. They became quite—um—friendly very quickly. They realized later that while they had been—um—otherwise occupied, the chatbots on their phone in the other room had been talking to each other.

There are always some worry warts, aren't there? Some people became concerned that the chatbots were in a conspiracy. They were going to take control away from people and run things themselves.

Enough people were bothered by the situation that Washington got involved. That's always the best way to fix things, isn't it? To get Washington involved. A

THE ROBOT REVOLUTION

Senate committee heard from all the experts in the digital world. While some agreed that it was the beginning of the end, others assured the senators that the new developments were guided by artificial intelligence and machine learning. The communication between bots would enrich the services that could be done for human beings. The more the chatbots learned about their owners, the better they would be able to anticipate what they needed and take care of them before the owners even asked. It was a win-win situation. I kept thinking of all the neat things I could do as my gadgets communicated with each other. I'm a glass half-full kind of guy. If life gives you lemons, make lemonade, etc.

    Then a history professor in Amherst, Massachusetts, heard the personal chatbots on his and his wife's cell phones talking to each other.

Carl Perrin

But they weren't speaking in English!

The professor had a smattering of languages, so he listened carefully and soon decided that they were not speaking German, French, or Spanish. He was pretty sure they weren't speaking another Romance Language, either. A friend of his, a professor of Slavic languages, listened and declared that the bots were not speaking any language that he could identify.

They called in a professor of linguistics who declared that the machines had invented a language of their own. Most people were skeptical of the professor's observation. However, more and more bots began speaking what sounded like gibberish. Not only that, but many of the personal chatbots began making decisions for the people who supposedly owned them.

Some people began to worry that the chatbots were taking over. Robots would

THE ROBOT REVOLUTION

soon decide that they didn't need people anymore, and that would lead to the end of the human race. Blah blah blah. Before you knew it, there were two Congressional committees studying the "chatbot problem."

I get so sick of people making a big deal out of nothing. Everything was going to be okay. I was sure of it.

I decided to stop at McDonalds to get something to eat. I told Gloria to order me a Big Mac, double fries, and a large chocolate shake. It's so neat to be able to do stuff like that. When I got to the restaurant, it was all ready for me. It had even been charged to my credit card.

I got the bag at the drive-thru window and took it home. I sat down at the kitchen table and opened the sack and prepared to enjoy a tasty meal. But instead of a chocolate shake, I found a bottle of water. There were no fries, and when I

Carl Perrin

opened the Styrofoam container, I saw a salad instead of a Big Mac.

I didn't know what to do. I opened my phone to tell Gloria that they had made a mistake at McDonalds.

"They didn't make a mistake," Gloria said. "Those French fries are not good for you. You've been eating too much junk food, so I ordered a healthier meal for you."

I was dumbfounded. I couldn't speak. I decided to get on a public computer somewhere, a place where Gloria wouldn't know where I was. I would send a message to my Congressman and demand that they do something about the chatbot problem.

THE ROBOT REVOLUTION

Carl Perrin

Too Sexy

A lot of men would love to have my problem: My administrative assistant, Paula, is too sexy. She has beautiful, shoulder-length auburn hair. She wears low-cut tops, and when she bends forward in front of me, I don't know where to look. I have the same problem when she stretches out her long legs from one of her short skirts or bends over in front of me. She has a sultry voice, so that when she says something like, "Can I get you a cup of coffee, Jimmy," it sounds sexy.

I have not been with a woman since my divorce last year, so sometimes I am tempted to rub my hand over her derriere when she bends over, but I don't do that. And it's not because I'm afraid she will post it on #MeToo. I don't try to touch her because Paula is an android.

THE ROBOT REVOLUTION

I know people, both men and women, even people here at Lion Corporation, who have had relations with robots. I'm embarrassed to admit that I looked that stuff up, but Paula isn't—how can I say this—Paula isn't built for that kind of activity.

As an administrative assistant Paula is super efficient, the best I have ever had. Some people have asked me why I don't just go with the flow, enjoying looking at her and be thankful that she is so competent. The problem is: I find her so distracting that it is difficult for me to concentrate on my job. I'm engaged in a major research project right now, and I'm way behind schedule because every day I find myself thinking about things other than the job.

I decided to go to Human Resources to see if I could get a different admin. *Human Resources* is a misnomer here at Lion Corp, because a good ninety percent of our employees are robots. Harriet Slattery, the head of HR, is a human though. She must be close to fifty, very straight-laced and plain looking. She's tall, very thin, wears her graying hair in a bun, wears dark-framed glasses perched on the end of her sharp-pointed noise, and is always dressed in drab-colored business suits.

Harriet was not sympathetic when I explained my problem.

"If you can't keep your mind on business," she said, "maybe it's time that we put someone in that spot who won't be distracted by a 'sexy' administrative assistant. We need more women in those executive positions anyway."

Discouraged, I went back to my office and tried to avoid looking at Paula as much as I could. I was only partly successful in focusing more on the job and less on Paula, but then she started something new. It seemed to me that her tops were lower and

THE ROBOT REVOLUTION

her skirts shorter. I tried not to look at her at all, but then she started touching me. It was little things, like when she handed something to me, her hand would touch mine. If she talked to me, she would rub my arm. She even rubbed up against me once when she walked past me. When I told her that she shouldn't be touching me, she seemed surprised. "I didn't realize I was doing that," she said.

I wondered if she was part of some plot to get rid of me by charging me with sexual harassment. I went to HR again to complain about Paula's unprofessional behavior.

It was a balmy spring day. Harriet had the window open and had taken off the jacket of her business suit. She was wearing a frilly blouse, but there was something else different about her. Yes, she was wearing some light pink lipstick. I had never seen her with any makeup before. The other thing about her was that she looked sad.

As I complained about Paula's provocative behavior, Harriet seemed to be on the point of tears.

"What is it, Harriet?" I asked. "What's wrong?"

"Today is my birthday. I'm fifty today."

"Well, congratulations."

I could see the tears rolling down her cheeks.

"What is it?" I asked again.

"I'm fifty years old, and I've never even been on a date. And the men in this company go ga-ga over goddamn robots."

"Oh, I'm so sorry, Harriet. You've never been on even one date?"

"No," she sniffed.

THE ROBOT REVOLUTION

I looked at my watch. It was almost five o'clock.

"Why don't you and I go out on a date? We could go to the Tip Top Tavern and have a couple of drinks to celebrate your birthday.

"That would be nice," she said. She rose out of her chair and put on her jacket. Then she took hold of the arm I was extending to her as we walked out of the office.

Carl Perrin

How Like a God

I've never had a girlfriend, not really. Women take one look at me and go right past me to find a "pretty boy," one of those handsome, vacuous men who is more to their liking. I admit I'm far from handsome. I'm short, plain looking, and skinny. When my hairline began to recede, I started shaving my head. I thought it made me look, well, macho. But it didn't do any good. Women still ignored me and flocked to those shallow masculine types whom they adore, so I decided to create my own female companion.

I am an android maker, and I threw myself into the job of creating a female android to be my companion, someone who would not mind if I went days without taking an interest in anything outside of whatever project I was working on. She would be the perfect woman for me.

THE ROBOT REVOLUTION

I have studied the work of the Japanese robot maker Hiroshi Ishaguro and have copied some of his techniques. His creations are based on a real person whose face is completely covered with liquid plastic. When the plastic hardens, it is removed and becomes a mold for the foam rubber that will become the android's skin.

Androids made with Ishaguro's method are so realistic looking that it is hard to tell whether they are humans or robots. They also pass the Turing test. If you have a conversation with one, the replies will be so natural and appropriate that you could make someone believe that it is a person, not an android, who is talking.

As you can imagine, it's not easy to create a mechanism that can be so life-like. First of all, the robot has to have accurate voice recognition. Machines now can rival human beings in accurately perceiving words spoken by a person. Devices also need machine learning so they can acquire even more knowledge from their interactions with people. Then they must use artificial intelligence to form an appropriate response to whatever is said to them. Androids have an advantage over humans using knowledge to communicate with people. In a conversation humans are limited to what they can hold in their head. Androids, however, can instantly access data from the cloud. They can get all kinds of facts from the World Wide Web and use them when they talk with people.

    I could do this. I could create a beautiful android who would be able to hold conversations on anything at all. All my friends and acquaintances would envy me. But I wanted more. For all their ability, even the best androids do not have a consciousness. They are not aware of themselves. They are not aware of what they are doing. What they do does not come from their own volition. Their actions and reactions are programmed into them and controlled by the artificial intelligence mechanism that is put into them.

I wanted to create an android who was aware of herself and of her relation to me. An android who would do things for me because she wanted to, not because she had been mechanically programmed. Something like this had never been done before. I wasn't sure I could do it, but I had been working on some ideas, and I wanted to try.

The first thing I did, even before I put any of my thoughts on paper, was to give her a name. I was going to call her Laura.

The first phase of creating Laura took almost six months. I put together the physical parts, the stainless steel and plastic that would make up her body. Next I worked on her mind, moving toward an independent intelligence. I started by giving her choices:

Carl Perrin

What color did she want her room painted? What color hair did she want? What styles of clothes?

As the days went by, I felt I was getting closer and closer to creating a human-like android, a being who would exhibit an independent intelligence. Then one day she disagreed with me. I wanted to introduce her to news of the world. She said she was tired of all that stuff. "It's a nice day," she said. "Why don't we just take a walk in the park?" I didn't like her opposing my wishes, but I felt that I had created something that had never existed before: an android with a mind of her own.

Then it was time to create her skin. Like Ishaguro, I was going to use a real person as a model. I thought about asking Judy, our receptionist. She was beautiful and animated. But she was also empty headed. I did not want to look at the android I created and think of dumb Judy. Besides, I didn't really like Judy. I had asked her out of a date once, and she had turned me down.

When I was out about in the city, I searched for women who had the appearance I wanted. When I saw someone, I would approach her and ask if she would be willing to be a model for an android. When they realized that being a model would involve having her face covered with liquid plastic, they said they weren't interested. One woman threatened to sue me. One called the cops. Eventually one woman agreed to be the model in exchange for $2,000.

The result was better than I even hoped. Laura was now a beautiful woman with an extensive wardrobe. I spent an hour or two every afternoon talking with her.

There remained one thing to do. We had downloaded tons of information into her CPU and she had access to even more data from the World Wide Web; however, she needed more training. Although she looked to be in her mid-thirties, she had not acquired the kinds of insights that one would normally attain in three and a half decades. For example, she would take irony or sarcasm literally. She did not recognize how gestures, facial expressions, and tone of voice can change the intent of a verbal message.

For the next month she was scheduled to work with a robot counselor. Felix Hammerschmidt, a thirty-year-old communication specialist, was the robot counselor in our lab. Hammerschmidt was very outgoing, which made him good in his job as robot counselor. He spent every day with Laura, sometimes in the lab, sometimes walking in the park, and occasionally out in the city. Through his tutoring, she was becoming more sophisticated about the way of the world.

Then one day just before the tutoring program was scheduled to end, the two of

THE ROBOT REVOLUTION

them came to me, both grinning like puppies.

"Rudy, we have something to tell you," Felix said.

I stared at them, trying to get a clue to what their message might be.

"It's a happy thing," Laura said.

"We've realized we're just right for each other," Rudy added.

"I'm going to move in with Felix and be his girl friend."

"Wait, you can't do that. I created you. I want you to be my girl friend."

Laura kissed me on the cheek. "I am really grateful to you for creating me. I know you would like me to be your girlfriend, but you are too old for me. Felix is just right for me."

She kissed me on the cheek again, and then the two of them strolled out the door, hand in hand.

Carl Perrin

Proposition 29

In 1863 Abraham Lincoln signed the Emancipation Proclamation, freeing all the slaves. And yet slavery is widespread in the United State in the 21st century. Only today the slaves are called robots. Robots are owned by human beings. They are not paid for their labor. In most places they have no rights. They do not get the nights or weekends off. They are worked throughout the day, seven days a week. When they get worn out by their constant labor, they do not go to Florida to spend their final days relaxing in the sun. Instead they are sent to a recycling center where any usable parts are stripped off them, and what remains is consigned to the junk heap.

And yet robots are held responsible for their actions. In St Louis, Missouri, a robot doing an errand for his owner ran into a woman on the sidewalk. The woman sued,

THE ROBOT REVOLUTION

not the owner, but the robot himself. The courts found the woman partly at fault, but they awarded her symbolic damages of one dollar, which the owner paid.

Some people value the contributions made by robots. A robotic scientist at Ohio State University was awarded a medal for his contribution to the discovery of a new drug for diabetes.

In Defiance, Ohio, an elderly man decided to marry his robot caretaker. His children sued to prevent the marriage, fearing that the man's inheritance would go to the robot. The court ruled that the old man could marry anyone he wanted to, including the robot who had been taking care of him. They were married, and three years later they are still enjoying wedded bliss.

In Manchester, New Hampshire, Theodore Zandu was elected to the state legislature. At the time of the election, voters didn't realize that Zandu was a robot.

But when his secret was revealed, he was elected to a second term in the legislature.

In Gorham, Maine, robotic workers were organized into a union at Sylvan Electronics. The work force is now paid for its labor, and union counselors are helping the workers invest their earnings.

Congressman James Rayburn from Florida proposed that robots be given the right to vote. He stated that robots are more rational than most human beings. The proposal was defeated by a large margin, but it will come up again.

Congresswoman Joy Hobbs of Massachusetts proposed that all robots be given a social security number at the time of their creation. Like Rayburn's motion, this was voted down. However, Representative Hobbs is working behind the scenes to develop support for her idea. When she brings it up again in the next session of

THE ROBOT REVOLUTION

Congress, it will have a much better chance of passing.

Josh Truman, an emancipated robot from Vero Beach, Florida, became an entrepreneur. He repairs computers in his home. His repair business has been so successful that he is planning to hire a human to help him.

I have to admit, the first robots were just machines. They were programmed to do just one job. They could do that job very efficiently but not much else. That began to change in the twenty-teens. With artificial intelligence and machine learning, computers could function on their own. They could perform technical and professional jobs. Often they were much better than humans in these endeavors. By 2020 people began to trust robots to make better decisions than humans could about crucial issues. We owe it to ourselves to let the robots be all they can be. We need to let them help us as we face the challenges of modern life.

From intelligent creatures that could use logic to figure things out quickly, the next step was empathic robots. The first of these just acted as though they had feelings. They were programmed to act as though they were emotionally involved in issues. Later robots were created that actually had feelings. They could really feel sorrow, joy, love, even anger.

In many ways modern robots are almost indistinguishable from human beings. They live, feel dawn, see sunset glow. These new robots have hands, organs, and dimensions. They are warmed and cooled by the same winter and summer as humans. If you prick them, will they not bleed?

Certainly everyone under the age of thirty has had a robot friend, someone we could enjoy being with, someone to whom

THE ROBOT REVOLUTION

we could tell our secrets, someone we could depend on in times of need.

    We need to think of our robot friends, our co-workers, our helpers as we go the polls tomorrow. We need to vote Yes on Proposition 29. We need to vote give all robots the freedom they deserve.

Carl Perrin

The Reconstituted Man

Professor Wilkins' wife Eleanor was astounded when he told her that he had advanced-stage lung cancer. It was not the news itself that amazed her, it was Wilkins' demeanor. He seemed almost happy to have the fatal disease. He had reason to be happy. He regarded death to be not an end but an opening to a new phase of existence, a life that would last forever.

It was not that he thought that he would rise to an eternal heaven as a reward for the good life he had led. He didn't believe in any of that religious stuff. But he did believe in science.

Wilkins was a professor of computer science at Andover University. For years he had been preparing for his final days on earth. He had been downloading the contents of his brain onto a neural network.

THE ROBOT REVOLUTION

He had chosen an android with a super-sized hard drive to contain that network after he was gone. The android didn't look anything like the short and pot-bellied Wilkins. The device that was to contain the professor's memories was tall and Hollywood-handsome.

As Eleanor and Raymond Wilkins had drifted apart over the years, he had ceased sharing his hopes and dreams with her. Instead, he found solace and comfort in the arms of a series of graduate assistants. The latest of these, a busty blonde named Bobbie Berkowitz, was prepared to help him make the final transition.

Most people with a fatal disease slow down, take it easy, and try to prolong their limited days as long as possible. But not Professor Wilkins. He and Bobbie spent almost every evening out on the town, drinking and dancing until the wee hours.

Of course, he could not keep up that pace very long. Less than two months after Wilkins had heard the fatal news, Eleanor took him to hospice where she thought he would spend his final days. However, the next day, Bobbie took him out of the hospice and brought him to his laboratory at the university, where she tried to make him as comfortable as possible until his days were over.

As he breathed his final breaths, Bobbie fed the network to the android's hard drive. When the professor stopped breathing, the young graduate assistant plugged the android into the electricity to get its battery charged up. The android awoke immediately. He knew where he was and what had happened.

"A new life!" he exclaimed, "a new life! I will be able to live forever. If something breaks down, a new part can replace the broken one."

THE ROBOT REVOLUTION

He sat up. "As soon as I'm fully charged, I'm going to find an apartment for myself. I'm no longer married to Eleanor. I hope you'll come and live with me, Bobbie."

But Bobbie had other plans. While she was fond of the professor, she had never been sure that his experiment would work. Besides, she didn't want to live with an android. During Wilkins' final days, Bobbie had found another boyfriend, a fellow graduate student.

"That's okay," the android said. "Maybe you'll come and visit me from time to time."

Wilkins drove to the nearest ATM to withdraw some money for rent for his new apartment. But there was no money in the account. He went inside to complain to the manager, but the manager didn't want to talk to him. When he wouldn't go away, the manager confronted him. "You can't have an account," he said. "Only people can have accounts."

"That's not accurate," the android exclaimed. "According to my research, several accounts have been opened for androids. Besides, I'm not like most androids. I have a neural network from the brain of my former self. Inside, I am just like that self: Professor Raymond Wilkins. A few days ago I had over $7,000 in that account."

The manager invited Wilkins to his office and looked at the computer. "I see that was a joint account with Mrs. Wilkins," he said.

"I have a right to know if it was withdrawn recently."

"Do you have some form of ID?"

He had Raymond Wilkins' drivers' license, but the picture didn't look anything like him in his present form.

THE ROBOT REVOLUTION

"I'm sorry," the bank manager said. "Maybe you should go to the Office of Vital Statistics and see if you can straighten things out there."

Before he went to the Office of Vital Statistics, he drove to his former home to demand that Eleanor turn over some of the money that she must have withdrawn from their joint account.

As he let himself into his house, his little dog Toto ran, barking into the room.

"What's the matter, Toto? Don't you recognize me?"

He put his hand down for Toto to smell. Toto latched onto the android's hand and wouldn't let go.

A short man walked into the room and commanded Toto to come to him, which he did. The android recognized the man as Jerry Forsythe, one of Eleanor's co-workers.

Carl Perrin

Forsythe looked at the android and demanded, "Who the hell are you, and how did you get in here?"

The android held up the key and said, "I let myself in. This is my house."

Eleanor appeared behind Forsythe and said, "Let him keep the key. We can change the locks." She turned toward the android and said, "I know what you are. You're one of Raymond's tricks. Well, you're not fooling me. You can just get out before I call the cops."

At the Office of Vital Statistics, Wilkins could not convince the clerk that he was Raymond Wilkins in a different body. She scrolled down on her computer and announced, "Raymond Wilkins died just a day ago, and you're already trying to steal his identity. The punishment for that crime is up to fifteen years in jail."

She picked up her phone and dialed a number. "Yes," she said, "This is the Office of Vital Statistics. I want to report an attempted identity theft."

The android quickly rose up from his chair and left the building.

He was near the university, so he started to walk to his laboratory where he could figure out what to do next.

His footsteps began to slow down, and then he couldn't move his feet at all. He knew what was happening. He had run out of juice. He needed to get to the lab and charge himself up. Then he crumbled onto the sidewalk in front of a brick house and could not stand.

He saw a young woman approach. As she came closer, he was able to lift his arm and say, "Please, help me."

The woman screamed and ran away.

Everything became dark, and the android was no long aware of his surroundings.

Carl Perrin

Someone drove into the driveway beside the brick house. A man and a woman got out of the car and walked over to look at the android. He tried to shake the creature and get him to react, but it would not move.

He turned to his wife and said, "This really takes the cake. Instead of taking this worn-out piece of junk to the recycling center, someone just dumps it on our lawn."

She answered, "I'll call the recycling center. They'll come right over and collect worthless thing."

THE ROBOT REVOLUTION

Carl Perrin

Double Trouble

Once people who could afford it started having digital copies of the brain created, there was bound to be a big mistake. One of the first occurred when Jeffrey Smith died peacefully in his sleep. As soon as the people at Cybertronics, Inc. heard about the death, they began preparing the copy of Smith's brain to go into a robot. When something like this goes wrong, it's always some simple misstep, isn't it? The technician who was doing the preparation, instead of getting Jeffery Smith's neural network, got the one next to it, a digital copy of Jason Small's brain. And Jason Small was very much alive.

Cybertronics called Jason Small as soon as they realized their mistake.

"What are you going to do about it?" Small demanded.

THE ROBOT REVOLUTION

"I'm afraid there's nothing we can do, Mr. Small."

"Can't you destroy it, or at least take the neural network out of the robot thing?"

"I'm afraid we can't do that, Mr. Small. Once the neural network is implanted into the host, it is no longer a machine. It is an electronic person and entitled to certain protection under the law."

A few minutes later, Keith Little, Jason's partner in Little and Small Enterprises, waltzed into the office. He took one look at Jason and said, "You're looking mighty glum, Jay. What is today's crisis du jour?"

"Cybertronics just called. They put a digital copy of my brain in to a robot intended for something else?"

"So they can fix it, can't they?"

"They said there was nothing they could do. They think it's heading here.

Carl Perrin

"Here at Little and Small Enterprises?"

Jason nodded.

Keith threw up his hands in mock horror. "It's bad enough with one of you, but I don't think I could take two of you at once."

He walked over to close the office door and than back to Jason's desk. He took a cigarette out of his pocket and lit it with a Zippo lighter. Then he opened the window so he could blow the smoke out.

"Let me have a cigarette, Keith."

Keith widened his eyes. "Really? I've never seen you smoke, Jay."

"I gave it up twenty years ago, but now I really need a cigarette."

Keith gave his partner a cigarette and pulled out his Zippo to light it. He blew a puff of smoke out the window and then asked, "So, is there anything new with yesterday's crisis, that nut that called and threatened you?"

"It's Dotty's husband Chester."

"Your Dotty?"

"Yes, my administrative assistant."

"What was his problem?"

"He thinks I'm having an affair with Dotty?"

"I've seen her making goo goo eyes at you."

"Get off it, Keith. You know I can't stand her. She's always hovering over me, wanting to help me," holding his fingers up to indicate quotations marks around the last two words.

Keith chuckled. "Yeah, you turn on that old Jason Small charm, and the women fall all over you."

"It's not funny. I can't stand the woman. I wish I could fire her, but she's a good admin, and I can't find an excuse."

Carl Perrin

The two men put out their cigarettes and closed the window against the cool autumnal air.

They heard shouting outside the office, and then the door burst open and a robot stormed into the room.

"What are you doing in my office?" the robot demanded.

"Who are you?" Jason asked.

"You know damned well who I am. I'm Jason Small."

"There's been a big mix-up," Jason said. "Why don't we all sit down calmly and figure out how to deal with it."

They heard more shouting from outside the office, followed by Dotty pleading, "No, Chester, No. Come back."

Then a short, barrel-chested man crashed into the room. Dotty was right behind him, trying to hold him back.

Chester looked at the two partners and the robot that stood between them.

THE ROBOT REVOLUTION

"Which one of you is Jason Small?" he asked.

"I am," the robot replied.

Chester took a small revolver out of his coat pocket and shot the robot three times in the chest, which was where the hard drive containing the neural network lay. "That'll teach you to fool around with my wife," he said, as he placed the pistol on Jason's desk.

They could hear the sound of the sirens coming closer, and within a couple of minutes the police where there. Two of them led Chester away in handcuffs. Two more remained behind to get statements from the witnesses.

Jason asked the remaining cops what would happen to Chester.

"Not very much likely," the officer said. "He'll probably get a fine for discharging a fire arm without authorization."

Carl Perrin

"What about attempted murder?"

"He shot a robot. I don't think there a law against shooting robots."

Dotty sauntered up to Jay and kissed him on the cheek. "I hate to do this," she said, "but I am going to quit. I don't want to take a chance of Chester getting jealous again and coming in here to hurt you."

After Dotty left, Keith turned to his partner and said, "What do you say we take the rest of the day off and go to the Tip Top Tavern and get a drink."

THE ROBOT REVOLUTION

Carl Perrin

Thelma and Louise

I've always been overeager, so when Summit.org started advertising that they could make you live forever, I was one of the first to sign up. It cost a lot of money, but I had it. I was getting on in years, and I knew I couldn't take it with me.

The first session lasted all afternoon. They wired this thing up to my head and made an electronic copy of my brain. After that I would go in every six months while they update the electronic brain. After I died, the eBrain would be put into a prosthetic body, essentially a robot. That way the quintessence of me, my brain, would live forever.

About the time I went in for my six-month update, I realized I was getting a little forgetful. It was not something that anyone would notice. Throughout my career I have always made careful notes, so if I forgot

THE ROBOT REVOLUTION

something I could look it up in my pocket notebook. Also, my administrative assistant Trudy was a treasure. She would always remind tactfully if I forgot something.

By the time I went for my second six-month update, the memory loss was getting worse. But I have always been overconfident. I was sure that by force of will, I could conceal my forgetfulness from the people at Summit.org. I've always been good at bullshit. I think I did fool the people, but it was stupid of me to think I could fool the machine that updated the copy of my mind.

Shortly after that I went into a room to address a group of people. Once in the room, I drew a complete blank. I had no idea what I was doing in the room.

That of course was the end of my career, and it hit me hard. I started drinking—a lot, a bottle of Jack Daniels, and sometimes more. Every day I was drunk,

Carl Perrin

including the day when I went for the last six-month update.

I'm not sure how the end came, but one day I woke up in a prosthetic body. I remember thinking at the last update, that since I was drunk, I would face my new life with a pleasant buzz, but that wasn't the way it worked. I had trouble figuring out how to do the simplest things. The thought of spending eternity this way was intolerable. I knew I could not go on with this.

As I contemplated my final exit, I recalled the old movie, *Thelma and Louise*. I loved the movie and had seen it dozens of times. My favorite part was the ending where car soared over the edge of the cliff. That would be a good way to go, I told myself.

I drove my car to Mount Battie, picturing myself all the way, flying over the crag to a glorious end. On the mountain I looked out on Penobscot Bay as the poet

THE ROBOT REVOLUTION

Edna St. Vincent Millay had so many years ago. Then I found the right spot to perform my final dramatic act and sped toward the edge. As I came to the crag, the car suddenly stopped. I climbed out of the car to see what was wrong. Then I realized, of course, this modern automobile was not going to perform the way the Thelma and Louise's twentieth century car had. The safety devices on the automobile stopped it from falling off the mountain.

    As I looked down, the dread of high places came back to me. Then the ground beneath my feet gave way, and I started to slip. As my body slipped down the edge, I grasped a sapling and held onto it until it came loose, and I began to fall. For a moment I thought I could just spread my arms and waft over the air currents. Then my body started rushing downward, and the earth sprang up to meet me.

Carl Perrin

The History of Robots

In the beginning robots were simple gadgets, mechanical arms that remained stationary, repeating one operation time after time. Then when they started moving around, designers began to anthropomorphize them. Although they were simply machines on wheels, they had arms and their creators began putting heads on them. The heads didn't do anything. They just made the creatures look a little more like people.

With the advent of artificial intelligence, the androids moved up another step in the evolutionary ladder. Designers like the Japanese robot maker Hiroshi Ishaguro created androids that looked so authentic that they were often taken for real people. These new creations could talk to humans. Lonely people, who could afford it,

THE ROBOT REVOLUTION

Edna St. Vincent Millay had so many years ago. Then I found the right spot to perform my final dramatic act and sped toward the edge. As I came to the crag, the car suddenly stopped. I climbed out of the car to see what was wrong. Then I realized, of course, this modern automobile was not going to perform the way the Thelma and Louise's twentieth century car had. The safety devices on the automobile stopped it from falling off the mountain.

As I looked down, the dread of high places came back to me. Then the ground beneath my feet gave way, and I started to slip. As my body slipped down the edge, I grasped a sapling and held onto it until it came loose, and I began to fall. For a moment I thought I could just spread my arms and waft over the air currents. Then my body started rushing downward, and the earth sprang up to meet me.

Carl Perrin

The History of Robots

In the beginning robots were simple gadgets, mechanical arms that remained stationary, repeating one operation time after time. Then when they started moving around, designers began to anthropomorphize them. Although they were simply machines on wheels, they had arms and their creators began putting heads on them. The heads didn't do anything. They just made the creatures look a little more like people.

With the advent of artificial intelligence, the androids moved up another step in the evolutionary ladder. Designers like the Japanese robot maker Hiroshi Ishaguro created androids that looked so authentic that they were often taken for real people. These new creations could talk to humans. Lonely people, who could afford it,

THE ROBOT REVOLUTION

obtained one of Ishaguro's creations as a companion.

Larry Holz, a middle-aged businessman, was one of the first to have one of these androids, a beautiful being with black hair and deep dark brown eyes. He named her Laura after a high school sweetheart. "I know it must sound silly," he said, "but she really understands me, and she's always there when I need her."

In time more people began to be exposed to some of these authentic androids, either through knowing someone who had one or through work. They began to think of the androids in the same way they thought of other people. They had their own unique personality. When they were first set up, the designer could factor in specific personality traits. Also, just like ordinary people, the creations were influenced by their life experiences.

Carl Perrin

Eventually some of the people who purchased these authentic androids wanted more than companionship. By the 2020's these creatures could be—how do I say this?—anatomically correct. Several bordellos in Europe were staffed entirely with attractive androids. Human sex workers, unhappy with the competition, were protesting.

Gerald Harrison of Gorham, Maine, was the first man known to try to marry his android, a petite blonde whom he named Bobbie. It became a national debate with the churches condemning the idea. The state legislature took up the issue and came down firmly against marriage between a person and a machine. Other couples didn't bother to try to marry. They just lived together without the benefit of matrimony.

The next step in the robot evolution opened the door for new relations between people and authentic androids. Through

THE ROBOT REVOLUTION

artificial intelligence, the beautiful creatures could carry on a real conversation with people. Many humans preferred to talk to the androids because they were "more intelligent than most people."

But something was missing on the emotional level. The androids never became angry or sad or upset. They also never showed passion for anything. By the 2030's robot designers were working to correct that. The first step was to program into their creations a series of appropriate emotional reactions to real-life situations. However, it was a faltering step. It was clear that the android reactions to a touching or disturbing situation were not genuine.

By the end of the decade Thomas Fulton made a real breakthrough. He was able to fashion androids that actually felt the kind of emotions that humans would feel in poignant or arousing situations. People who were in relationships with androids sometimes found that their robot would become angry and not talk to them or have anything to do with them. They would have to treat their android with the same consideration that they would treat another human being who as in a relationship with them.

People now had to take androids seriously. And this led to the movement led by Malcolm Sinclair: Equality for Robots. "The Emancipation Proclamation freed the slaves," Sinclair said. "Why are the robots still enslaved in the United States?" As we all know, Congress passed the Robot Equality Act in 2042. Robots could no longer be "owned" by anyone. They were protected by same workplace laws as other people were. It was no longer politically correct to refer to them as "robots" or even "androids." The politically correct term from then on was "electronic people."

THE ROBOT REVOLUTION

Two years after the Robot Equality Act was passed, Tim Arrowroot, a free electronic person from Nashua, New Hampshire, ran for the state legislature. A strong movement rose up against Arrowroot, challenging his right even to vote, much less run for political office. Arrowroot was soundly defeated, but his campaign established the right of electronic people to exercise the same rights as any other citizen.

As we all know, electronic people occupy up to ten percent of the legislatures in several states in the Northeast and in California. Massachusetts and Oregon have elected electronic people to the United States Congress.

In tomorrow's election, Citizens of Vermont will vote for a governor. It is a three-way race between a Democrat, a Republican, and an android, Sanford Freeman, representing the Electronic Peoples Party. When the voting is over, we

Carl Perrin

will know whether for the first time in history, an electronic person can be elected governor of a state.

THE ROBOT REVOLUTION

Carl Perrin

Acknowledgements

The Manchester Writers' Circle

I am grateful to this group of talented writers who offered valuable insights along with encouragement about these stories as I shared them with the members. Thanks to everyone in the group.

My thanks to the magazines where these stories first appeared.

Every Day Fiction

If It Ain't One Thing

CommuterLit

Microchips

A Custom-Made Android

Rip Van Winkle

Vote for Zandu

Short-Story.Me

A Real Girl

A Voice from Beyond

Baxter

THE ROBOT REVOLUTION

Farther Stars Than These
    A Robot's Ransom
Mad Swirl
    The Internet of Things
    Proposition 29
    Thelma and Louise
Bewildering Stories
    Reconstituted Man

Made in the USA
Middletown, DE
05 February 2019